KONSTANTIN STANYUKOVICH

Born in 1843 and son of a Vice-Admiral, Konstantin Stanyukovich seemed destined for a naval career. Sent to the Navy Cadet College he was unable to persuade his father to let him transfer to University. Instead he was sent on a long-range cruise 'so as to knock the nonsense out of his head'. He had already had eight poems published, but it was four years later before he finally left the navy to pursue his literary interests. Difficulties with censorship eventually led to a three-year administrative exile in Tomsk, Siberia, and it was there that he began to write his sea stories—the first Russian writer to devote attention to the navy and life at sea, and to create an authentic figure of a Russian sailor.

The crew of the Russian frigate *Osliaba*,

The corvette *Vitiaz* at Nagasaki, from *A History of Russian Sea Power*, 1974, by Donald W. Mitchell (*reproduced with the kind permission of André Deutsch*)

RUNNING TO THE SHROUDS

Nineteenth-century sea stories

by

Konstantin Stanyukovich

Translated from the Russian

by

Neil Parsons

FOREST BOOKS
LONDON ★ 1986 ★ BOSTON

PUBLISHED BY FOREST BOOKS
20 Forest View, Chingford, London E4 7AY, U.K.
61 Lincoln Road, Wayland, M.A. 01788, U.S.A.

First published 1986

Typset in Great Britain by Cover to Cover, Cambridge
Printed in Great Britain by A. Wheaton & Co Ltd, Exeter

Translation © Neil Parsons
Cover design © Ann Evans

British Library Cataloguing in Publication Data
Stanyukovich, Konstantin
    Running to the shrouds: six Russian sea stories.
    1. Title
    891. 73'3 (F)   PG3470.S73
    ISBN 0–948259–06–X

Library of Congress Catalog Card Number 86–081346

The publisher acknowledges the financial assistance of the Carnegie
Trust for the Universities of Scotland and also Glasgow University
Publications Department.

Contents

Translator's Note: When addressing their officers Russian sailors used the titles 'Your Honour', 'Your Excellency'. I have chosen 'Sir' in preference, as the Russian titles sound excessively quaint in English. The Russian patronymic commonly contracts in conversation; thus Ivan Ivanovich becomes Ivan Ivanych. First names have familiar and affectionate forms; thus Vladimir in 'The Joke' is at one point called Volodenka.

The stories are translated from Volumes 1 and 3 of the 6-volume Collection of Stanyukovich's works published in Moscow in 1959.

Introduction

Konstantin Stanyukovich (1843–1903), little known outside Russia, is remembered mainly for his *Sea Stories*, though they constitute a comparatively small part of his total output. He was, in fact, the only Russian writer of the nineteenth century to devote serious attention to the navy and life at sea. His *Sea Stories* were based upon his own experience as a naval officer in the years 1860–1863 and, apart from their not inconsiderable literary merits, they offer an unique insight into life and conditions in the Russian Navy in the years following the Crimean War. This is a particularly interesting period from several points of view: it saw a determined attempt to modernise the navy, the adoption of a new naval strategy, and a degree of real rapprochement with the United States, which was based upon shared suspicion of the great maritime powers, Britain and France.

*

Shortly before the Crimean War the Navy Ministry had passed under the direction of Grand Duke Konstantin Nikolayevich, a forward-looking, influential man who was genuinely interested in the sea. The lessons of the war were not lost on Konstantin, and once the war was over, Russia embarked upon a thorough overhaul of the navy. In the years 1855–1863, 130 steam-propelled warships were built, the vast bulk of them stationed in the Baltic, and in 1863 Russia began building ironclads. It was also realised that the Russian navy must maintain a presence on the high seas, for in the Crimean War Russian squadrons had been completely bottled up. Accordingly, once Kronstadt was felt to be secure with 9 screw-propelled ships-of-the-line, Konstantin recommended a shift of priority to commerce-raiders. The naval construction programme for 1860 reflects the new strategy very clearly—1860 saw the launching of 6 frigates, 3 corvettes, 6 clippers, but not a single ship-of-the-line.[1]

An essential part of the new programme was the institution of long-range cruises. To this end foreign coaling stations would need to be acquired, and it was this consideration, among others, that led Konstantin to seek a rapprochement with France and the United States. We learn from the story 'A Terrible Day' that convicts were transported from Siberia to Sakhalin for the express purpose of mining coal for ships of the Pacific Squadron. It is worth stressing, however, that these new frigates, corvettes and clippers were sailing ships in the full

---

1. Jacob W. Kipp, *Russian Naval Reformers and Imperial Expansion 1856–1863*, Soviet Armed Forces Review Annual I (ed. David R. Jones), Academic International Press, 1977, pp. 118–149 (p. 122).

meaning of the term; they were not armour-clad and their engines had a strictly auxiliary role. It is true that in the early '60s the Navy Ministry became worried by the emergence of ironclads and proceeded to convert some ships into ironclads. Even so, at this period there could be no question of cladding long-range ships designed to fulfil the role of commerce-raiders—this would have meant depriving them of their speed and manoeuvrability, their prime assets. The era of the armoured cruiser came with the '70s.

In the years following the Crimean War it was the Far East that primarily absorbed Russian naval energies, for only on the Pacific did Russia have free access to the seas. The policy of naval expansion in the Far East went hand in hand with Russian penetration of Central Asia and the empire-building activities of the Governor-General of Siberia, Count Muravyev. There was concern at growing British influence in Peking, and Admiral Putyatin's recommendations for a naval build-up in the area with a view to extracting territorial concessions from the Chinese represent a classic example of 'gunboat diplomacy'. In 1860 Russian warships moved towards the disputed Ussuri River region, effected a landing, and began building a naval station, Vladivostok. Russian rights in the area were confirmed by treaty. The story 'A Joke' portrays a Russian clipper moving up the Yangtse-Kiang River on a sweltering summer's day during the later stages of the Taiping Rebellion. The only ostensible purpose of the voyage (though not of the story) is 'to show the flag'.

It was Konstantin's aim that Russia should possess the third strongest navy. This aim was not, in itself, difficult to achieve—the real question was how poor a third was Russia going to be. Although Konstantin had Alexander's support for his policy, there was in Russia little awareness of the importance of maintaining a strong, modern navy, and the navy was still, in fact, being run on an inadequate budget. In 1862 Konstantin was appointed Viceroy in Warsaw, and there was considerable anxiety in naval circles that the new strategy would be discarded and the navy left to degenerate into something fit only for a boating-park. These fears were expressed in a remarkable, anonymous article which appeared in March 1863 in the journal *Vremya*. The article bore the title 'Does Russia need a navy?',[2] and argued passionately that an efficient, modern navy was absolutely vital to Russia's interests. Despite the cries for economy that were to be heard on all sides, there should certainly be no reduction in naval expenditure. In words which show that Russia, still smarting from the experience of the Crimean War, regarded England as the prime potential enemy, the article observed: 'The extraordinary might of England, the colossal dimensions of her trade, the healthy state of her finances, all this is a consequence of English command of the sea. Destroy this command, and today or tomorrow the star of that great nation will set; destroy it, and England will be a third-rate power!'[3] Nor was a confrontation with England necessarily something to be dreaded and avoided at all costs. Despite her huge and powerful navy, she was not invulnerable. A very telling illustration of the soundness of maintaining a commerce-raiding capability on the high seas was provided by the Confederate privateer *Sumter*, which was inflicting dramatic losses on Federal shipping.—'And what is the *Sumter*? A

2. 'Nuzhen li flot Rossii?', *Vremya*, March 1863, pp. 5–48.
3. Ibid., p. 8.

shoddy merchant steamer with a crew of 50, one cannon on a turning platform, a few guns along the sides, and undistinguished either by strength of construction or even by particular speed.'[4] The inference was obvious. If a makeshift mediocrity like the *Sumter* could escape capture and make the world sit up and take notice, what impression would a force of Russian clippers make! Built of the finest oak, possessing an armament of three large rotating guns and four rifled guns, able to carry a 12-day supply of coal and to travel at 13 knots, they would surely impress England more than an army of 100,000 men.

It was this same year (1863) which provided the most impressive demonstration of the practical application of the new naval strategy. In the period 1857–1863 the Baltic Fleet was divided into three squadrons. One was designated for the defence of Petersburg, while the other two (the so-called Atlantic and Pacific Squadrons) were intended to fulfil a strategic role on the high seas. The Atlantic Squadron under Rear-Admiral Lesovsky consisted of three frigates, two corvettes and a clipper, while the Pacific Squadron under Rear-Admiral Popov consisted of three corvettes, two clippers, and a screw gunboat.[5] In 1863 British and French protests against Russian policy in Poland excited fears in some official quarters that the maritime powers might again try joint or unilateral action against Russia. Accordingly, the Atlantic Squadron left Kronstadt on 29 July in great secrecy with the destination New York. The orders Lesovsky carried with him stated that his purpose 'consists, in the event of a presently forseeable war with the western powers, in acting against our enemies with all possible means available to you, inflicting maximum damage and losses to enemy trade by means of separate cruisers or mounting attacks with the whole squadron against weak and poorly defended points in enemy colonies'.[6] It is usually assumed that the Pacific Squadron's visit to San Francisco was also in direct obedience to government instructions. This is not the case. The whereabouts of the Pacific Squadron in the late summer and autumn of 1863 were unknown to the Navy Ministry and the government, and its sudden appearance in San Francisco on 1st October was as much a surprise to Petersburg as to Washington. Popov had merely been instructed earlier in the summer to be prepared for possible war with England and/or France, and he had decided on his own initiative that San Francisco represented the best and safest starting-base for hostile operations, should war break out.[7]

The visit by units of the Russian navy to the United States, as is well known, was welcomed by the American government (President Lincoln visited ships of the Atlantic Squadron on 16th September) and was widely hailed as a gesture of support for the Union cause. In fact, with Lee's repulse at Gettysburg on 3rd July, and the fall of the great fortress of Vicksburg a day later, the Confederacy was ultimately doomed, and neither British nor French recognition of the rebels would be forthcoming. Nevertheless, even at the end of 1863 there were few, indeed, who could be sure of this. We thus see in the naval visit an example of Russia and the United States drawing together in the face of a common threat.

4. Ibid., p. 32.
5. L. G. Beskrovnyy, Russkaya armiya i flot v XIX veke, Moscow, 1973, p. 507.
6. M. M. Malkin, Grazhdanskaya voyna v SShA i tsarskaya Rossiya, Moscow-Leningrad, 1939, p. 260.
7. Ibid., p. 250.

The Russian intiative was an astute one.

Cordial relations between the two countries continued. Following Karakozov's attempt on the life of Alexander II in 1866, Congress passed a resolution denouncing this act by 'an enemy of emancipation' (clearly imagining Karakozov as a Russian John Wilkes Booth), and even went as far as to order that its sentiments be expressed personally to the Tsar Liberator by a special representative. Gustavus Vasa Fox, Assistant Secretary to the Navy, was chosen to head the mission, and he decided to travel to Russia on the double-turret monitor USS *Miantonomoh*. This was something of a feat in itself, as such low-profile vessels had never before ventured outside coastal waters. Fox's mission to Russia was a great success,[8] and substantially facilitated the memorable Alaska purchase of 1867.

Throughout the '60s argument went on between those who advocated a defensive naval posture and those who wanted to see the creation of a true High Seas Fleet capabale of performing a full strategic role. The simple fact of the matter was that the unarmoured screw frigates, corvettes and clippers on which Stanyukovich had sailed were rapidly becoming obsolete. In 1864 an article appeared in the *Navy Magazine* entitled 'The Contemporary Importance of an Ironclad Navy'. Its author argued that 100m. roubles should be spent on the construction of an ocean-going fleet. Such an outlay, he insisted, 'is not a luxury, but a necessity—a sad one, perhaps, but one that is not open to doubt'.[9] The government, of course, was unwilling to spend anything like such a sum upon the navy. It was, in fact, coming to look upon the navy more and more as a mere extension of the army—that is, its role as defender of home waters was stressed at the expense of an independent strategic role. The promising developments in the navy in the years following the Crimean War were not sustained with anything like the determination one might have expected. In its failure to appreciate the importance of an independent strategic role for the navy and in allocating to it funds insufficient for its real needs the government displayed an all too typical shortsightedness and was to reap a bitter harvest here, as elsewhere.

*

Stanyukovich was born in Sevastopol in 1843, the son of a Vice-Admiral. As an 11-year old boy he witnessed the siege of Sevastopol, and even participated in its defence to the extent that he helped prepare lint for wounded soldiers and took it to dressing stations. He was evacuated with other members of his family to Simferopol in the late autumn of 1854. It is clear that with his background he was destined for a naval career and in November 1857 he entered the Navy Cadet College. Between October 1859 and October 1860 he had eight poems published—a fact which bears witness to his already strong literary inclinations. During the summer months of 1860 he sailed on the training ship *Oryol*, but then in October announced to his stunned father his intention to transfer to university. His father quickly arranged for his son to be sent immediately on one

8. For an account of Fox's mission to Russia see Ronald J. Jensen, *The Alaska Purchase and Russo-American Relations*, University of Washington Press, 1975, pp. 39–44.

9. Beskrovnyy, op. cit., p. 506.

of the recently instituted long-range cruises, 'so as to knock the nonsense out of his head'. Thus, on 18th October, six months before his final examinations, Stanyukovich embarked on the screw corvette *Kalevala*.[10] In March 1861 he was off Java, and in April in Shanghai. In July he went down with a serious fever and was transferred to hospital in Vladivostok. He was discharged from hospital early in December, and in 1862 he sailed on various ships, visiting San Francisco with Admiral Popov on the clipper *Abrek* in the September. In January 1863 he was sent to Saigon to join the clipper *Gaydamak*. On 4th August 1863 he was sent by Admiral Popov to Petersburg with important papers for the Navy Ministry. Travelling via China and Siberia he arrived towards the end of September —shortly before the Pacific Squadron made its suprise appearance in San Francisco. Stanyukovich now lost little time in making it clear to his father that he intended leaving the navy. He was officially retired in November 1864 with the rank of lieutenant, but this involved a complete break with his father and the beginning of an unsettled period in his life.

He first worked for 7–8 months as an elementary school teacher in a village in Vladimir Province and then, until the end of 1876, had a number of jobs, mostly in railway administration, which gave him wide experience of Russian life, necessitating, as they did, residence in such towns as Kursk, Taganrog, Rostov-on-Don. During these years he continued to pursue his literary interests and contributed to a number of journals. Towards the end of 1876 he moved to Petersburg and decided to try to live solely by his pen. In 1880 he became one of the editors of the journal *Delo*, and in December 1883 he bought it on instalments. However, he was not destined to enjoy it for long. In the '70s he had been clearly sympathetic to the Populist movement, was having increasing difficulties with the censorship, and was well known to the police. In April 1884 he was arrested and spent a year in the Peter-Paul Fortress. In May 1885 he was sentenced to three years' administrative exile in Siberia (Tomsk). There he was visited on a number of occasions by George Kennan, who wrote very warmly of him in his book.

It was in Tomsk that Stanyukovich began writing his *Sea Stories*. Siberian exile could occasionally be a blessing in disguise. It had a profound effect upon Dostoyevsky and it also gave rise to Korolenko's *Siberian Stories*. Siberian exile tore Stanyukovich away from purely Russian concerns and gave him the leisure to reflect upon those very different three years in his youth when he had sailed the oceans of the world. He was, of course, a respected literary figure—he had been writing for over twenty years—but with these stories of the sea he suddenly acquired a fame and popularity that he had never previously known, and it is for them that he is remembered.

It has already been stated that Stanyukovich was the first Russian writer to devote attention to the navy and life at sea. We cannot count Bestuzhev-Marlinsky's melodramatic buccaneers, nor even Goncharov's 'The Frigate *Pallada*', since we learn from Goncharov much about foreign cities but little indeed about the life of the sailors with whom he shared his voyage. But, of course, this unique distinction would not be enough in itself to merit more than a

10. Two years later (21 October 1862) the 18-year old Rimsky-Korsakov left Kronstadt on his long-range cruise, sending parts of his First Symphony from various ports to Balakirev for correction.

passing acknowledgement.

One is struck immediately by the authenticity of the stories. They were based upon personal experience, and he was not tempted to go beyond the era and the ships he knew. He is adept at describing the dangers and drama attendant upon life at sea—the raising, lowering and reefing of sails in different weather, the work of topsailmen clinging to swaying yards in the teeth of icy winds which threaten to tear them from their precarious perches to plunge headlong into a raging sea or be smashed upon the deck far below. 'A Brilliant Captain' has as its theme the mania for speed at drills at this period, especially in the presence of French or British warships.

Some stories are even more obviously linked with personal experience. 'The Dread Animal' is really a portrait—and by no means an admiring one—of his father, while 'The Restless Admiral'[11] is a portrait of the eccentric, yet able Admiral Popov under whom Stanyukovich had served directly. This story expresses towards its close a keen sense of the end of an age, of a past gone forever. Sanyukovich writes of those elegant warships he knew with a nostalgia which in British history we find in memories of the trade clippers—the 'ghosters', the 'China birds':

Many years have passed since those days. All those ships . . . have long been broken up and remain only in the memory of the old sailors who sailed on them on distant seas and learned their hard trade under the command of such dedicated teachers as the restless admiral. The wooden steam and sail fleet somehow disappeared quickly and was replaced by those multi-million rouble giant ironclads whose ungainly appearance offends the eyes of sailors of the old generation; they are like irons, with small, bare masts, or no masts at all, in place of the former elegant rigging—yet they carry formidable guns, possess rams and, thanks to their powerful engines, can travel at a speed hitherto undreamed-of.

Then there are the superb sea-pictures—sailing in the tropics under a trade-wind, the onset of squalls, storms in icy seas. And what must have been even more interesting to a largely land-locked and little-travelled people—the pictures of foreign ports, such as Hong Kong, Singapore, San Francisco.

Another prominent feature of the stories is their pervasive humanitarian spirit. He writes of the Russian peasant-sailor with understanding and respect. One of the most remarkable stories, from this point of view, is 'Issy'. It was first published in 'Russian Wealth' in 1894, when anti-semitism was even more than usually rife in Russia, and it is one of the very few works in 19th century Russian literature which has a Jew as its central figure—moreover, a Jew who is portrayed with total, albeit sometimes amused, sympathy. It is set 'in the distant past', the 1830s—a typical stratgem when a writer feared trouble from the censors. Yet, despite the dramatic final episode and some fine individual scenes, Stanyukovich endows his hero with rather too many virtues and introduces an element of sentimentality which makes for possibly too cloying a cocktail. Korolenko displays the same tendency towards sentimentality; with both men it is a feature of the progressive, humanitarian bias of their work.

11. These stories—*Groznyy admiral* and *Bespokonyy admiral*—are too long and uneven to be included in this volume.

Introduction

Someone said of Vivaldi that he had not written 500 concertos, but one concerto 500 times. The same man would perhaps have said, had he read Stanyukovich, that Stanyukovich had not written 50 or so sea stories, but one sea story 50 times! Of course, he would again have been deliberately confusing pattern and substance, but the point is clear enough. Stanyukovich does tend to rework the same material—a tyrannical captain or officer, a brutal bo'sun, the dangers of working on the topyards, the smart outline of a clipper or frigate with her three masts set slightly back and a white or gold stripe running round her sides, sudden squalls, the staunch courage of the Russian seaman—such motifs reoccur quite regularly, and they occur the more obviously because Stanyukovich could be regarded as an exponent of what we have come to call *faction*. If one compares him with his contemporary, Joseph Conrad, one is immediately struck by a clear difference: Stanyukovich's stories have, as a rule, a weak story-line. In the 'sixties he had published *ocherki* (essays or studies) based on his naval experiences, and his later stories still bear, to a degree, the imprint of the *ocherk*. Not only are the stories rooted in a particular epoch, but they have as one of their prime concerns the faithful evocation of that brief period in Russian naval history characterised by the long-range cruises of wooden, screw-propelled sailing ships.

The 1880s and 1890s saw a flowering of the short story in Russia. If Korolenko with his *Siberian Stories* and his idealistic vagrants enlarged the horizons of Russian literature and brought to the depressed generation of the 1880s a romantic 'breath of fresh air', then Stanyukovich brought 'a sea breeze'—a breeze that came not from the enclosed waters of the Baltic or the Black Sea, but from the wide oceans beyond. And with that breeze came a new figure—that of the Russian sailor. Stanyukovich possessed a rare gift for dialogue; he had the ability to make his characters spring into life when they speak. Novikov-Priboy, perhaps the best-known of Russia's writers of the sea, readily acknowledged Stanyukovich's achievement: 'In essense Stanyukovich was the first to create the figure of the Russian sailor—a true son of the people ... After Stanyukovich many writers of the time wrote about Russian sailors, but not one of them succeeded in really revealing to the reader the heart and soul of the Russian sailor, his love for the sea and the navy.'[12]

Russian history is a bleak picture. Only occasionally is its gloom relieved by glimmers of light. Stanyukovich's stories are set in one such period, believed by many to herald a new day. Though written at a very different time, there is in them much of the atmosphere of the early 1860s, the years of the 'Great Reforms'. They thus acquire in retrospect a poignant, even poetic quality. This impression of poetry is reinforced by the sense of adventure and of boundless horizons which the sea supplies, by the delicate beauty of the ships in which he sailed, and, not least, by the decent instincts of the man himself.

Perhaps Stanyukovich had a harsh father. By sending him to sea his father did not succeed in 'knocking the nonsense out of his head', as he had hoped to do, but he *did* enrich Russian literature—and for that we should be grateful to him. But for those three years in Alexander's navy, it is very doubtful whether Stanyukovich would be more than a name on the long roll of honour of the 19th-century Russian intelligentsia; as it is, his trim ship sails on.

12. Novikov-Priboy, *Sochineniya*, 1950, Vol. V, p. 335.

A Brilliant
Captain

I

It was after eight o'clock on a September morning.
The Toulon roads were becalmed. The sun's heat had
not yet become oppressive.

The captain of the *Knight*, which was anchored near the
flagship of a French squadron, had just received the usual morning
reports and remained on the bridge, admiring the graceful
lines, tall masts, snow-white funnel and gleaming white deck of
his fine corvette.

Lieutenant-captain Rakitin was a young officer who was still
enjoying the honeymoon of his first command. His was one of
the best warships of the Baltic Fleet, and he took great pride in
the faultless order, the astounding cleanliness of his ship, and the
'ideal' speed with which drills were performed on board her.
Indeed, the *Knight* evoked the admiration even of foreign sailors.

It was a period of renewal in the fleet as well. Corporal
punishments had just been abolished. The captain was capable
of exercising his authority without cruelty, and his 'lads', as he
called the sailors, strained at their tasks. In the pursuit of 'ideal'
speed at drills they risked injuries and even their lives to satisfy
their brilliant captain's pride and desire to excel. They would not
let the *Knight* down.

Very smartly dressed in white, a slim, well-built, fair-haired
man close on thirty, handsome, with a self-confident face and
silky, light-brown moustache and sideburns, Rakitin took the
glass and looked at the French flagship. An exultant smile played
upon his face.

He put the glass aside and, screwing up his blue eyes, remarked
to the officer of the watch, midshipman Lazunsky:

—Looks like the French will have sail drill today.

—What about us, Vladimir Nikolaich?—asked the midshipman
cheerfully and respectfully.

—Of course.

—The French will be left 'dragging their tails' again, Vladimir Nikolaich!—the midshipman said excitedly, his young, beardless face wreathed in the smile of a conqueror.

But to Rakitin, who was very jealous of the dignity of his position, it suddenly seemed that the midshipman was being familiar, engaging in conversation with him. So he cut him short, saying rather sharply:

—The signalman must keep his eyes on the admiral's mizzen topmast!

—Aye-aye, sir, he's watching it!—the midshipman replied, immediately serious.

—You watch it too. Don't miss the signal.

—Aye-aye, sir. We won't miss it!—the somewhat offended midshipman replied even more seriously, assuming a professional tone of voice. And despite the fact that the signalman had not lowered the spyglass from the admiral's ship, the midshipman yelled at him:

—Keep a close watch on the admiral!

'What are you yelling for?!'—thought the signalman and shouted:

—Aye-aye, sir! I'm watching!

The captain did not leave the bridge but kept looking at the flagship's quarter-deck, where the admiral was walking up and down. He was a short, thin, elderly man with a hooked nose and small beard, and was wearing a long dark-blue uniform frockcoat, under wich was a snow-white shirt with turn-down collars. He was an unusually amiable and polite man, and an Orleanist, though he was serving under Napoleon III.

Rakitin was plucking impatiently at one of his sparse sideburns in anticipation of the *Knight*'s triumph. Yes, indeed! Several times already the *Knight* had aroused the professional envy and national displeasure of foreign sailors and gratified the pride of the brilliant Russian captain.

Whenever the *Knight* anchored in roads in the presence of a French or English squadron, Rakitin, observing the politenesses of international etiquette, would, upon the signal of the foreign admiral, order the same exercises performed on board the *Knight* as were being carried out by the foreign squadron. And in most cases the Russian corvette was the winner. All on board her were overjoyed. Even the doctor and the priest exulted at the fact that on the corvette sails were hoisted or furled a minute or a half-minute sooner than on the French or English ships.

II

—Signal!—the signalman yelled at the top of his voice.

Three little bundles had been run up the mizzen topmast of the flagship *Terrible* and fluttered out as signal flags aloft: 'Set all sails!'

The same second answering signals were raised on all the ships of the French squadron, and French words of command broke the silence of the roads.

—Whistle all hands on deck! Set the sails!—the midshipman shouted in an unnaturally loud, excited and squeaky voice, which he tried in vain to lower.

Whistles sounded along with the voices of bo'suns and petty officers.

The crew rushed to their places like a startled herd. The officers came running headlong out of the wardroom and sped to their masts. The old senior navigator hurried to the bridge at a trot, while his junior swept past him and took hold of the minute-glass to time the operation.

The *Knight*'s first lieutenant, Vasily Leontyevich, a small, round, fresh-faced man past thirty years of age, was already on the bridge. He was leaning his whole body over the rails, his short legs planted apart.

Everything became hushed.

—Topmen to the shrouds! To the tops and cross-trees!— came Vasily Leontyevich's loud, brisk, almost challenging order, delivered in a rich baritone voice. With that command his quick, brown eyes, like those of a young mouse, glanced at the 'Frenchman' to see whether they were on the shrouds there yet.

No, they weren't! Thank God!

The *Knight*'s topmen were already rushing like men possessed along the taut shrouds. Only their bare heels could be glimpsed. Some were already on the tops, others were clambering higher— to the cross-trees, while the French sailors were still running to the shrouds.

And the quick, lively 'Top', as Vasily Leontyevich was known on the foredeck, yelled more impatiently:

—Out along the yards!

White shirts ran out along the top and topgallant yards, holding on to the cross-pieces with one hand for balance. They moved as quickly as if they were running along the ground, not along round, transverse beams—the yards, the middle of which hung

at a terrifying height above the deck and whose ends were over
the sea. The sailors seemed oblivious of the fact that the slightest
carelessness could mean falling off and smashing your head on
the deck or plunging into the sea never to come up again.

—Away with the sheets! Away from the tops and cross-trees!
The first officer's voice was more nervous and impatient.

The captain had not taken his eyes off the yards and could
hardly restrain his agitation. To him disgrace seemed imminent:
the *Knight* would not outdo the French.

—How many minutes?—he shouted in a shaking voice.

—Two and a half!—the junior navigation officer replied.

'What are those scoundrels dawdling for!'—thought Rakitin,
as though forgetting the speed and daring with which the sailors
were performing their difficult and dangerous task.

—Vasily Leontich! How much longer?—he exclaimed with
reproach.

—The men are straining every nerve as it is!—Vasily Leontyevich replied.

Another endless minute . . .

From top to bottom, along the sides and aft along the jib-
boom the *Knight* was clothed in canvas, resembling a gigantic
bird with lowered wings.

Silence reigned on the corvette as before.

A minute later the sails had been set on the ships of the French
squadron too.

The captain's triumph, however, was not complete. He was
angry. His pride had been wounded. Very much so! Today the
sails had not been set with the usual fabulous speed; it had taken
forty seconds longer, and the *Knight* had only beaten the French
by a minute.

—Order the crew to line up, Vasily Leontyevich.

—Yes, sir!

A minute later the sailors were standing at attention.

Rakitin, his head raised, came to the middle of the assembled
men with quick, purposeful steps. All eyes were fixed on him. On
the strained faces of the sailors there was dejection. For several
seconds Rakitin said nothing, screwing up his eyes and looking
at a sailor standing opposite him. The young topman's eyes
bulged even wider and more vacantly at the captain.

—I didn't expect it of you, lads! You made a right mess of it
today. Dawdled!—the captain uttered in a severe, gloomily
solemn voice.

And the sailors seemed to feel a sense of guilt. Their faces became even more strained. The captain was well satisfied with the effect he was having and went on in a softer voice:

—Watch now! . . . Don't let yourselves down and don't let me down in front of the French. I'm sure . . . I know you're good lads . . .

—We'll do our best, sir!—the sailors roared with a sense of relief.

The captain gave the order to disperse, reassured that his 'lads' would not let him down and that they appreciated his words.

III

The sailors regarded Rakitin as a 'great captain' so far as they were concerned. They were overjoyed to get a breathing space after the former captain, a typical bully unsparing in his use of the lash as a means of punishment. The new one, though he exhausted them with drills and speed far more than his predecessor, was nevertheless 'decent'. He seldom had recourse to physical measures and then only 'within reason', did not much approve of officers engaging in 'beatings', and was not over-concerned about drunkenness ashore.

Though they hardly knew what it was like to rest and worked like men possessed, the sailors actually believed that they had 'made a mess of it' and that they could try harder. The old bo'sun Terentich, stirred by the captain's words, spoke to the sailors on the foredeck:

—You try harder, you devils! Don't let the captain down in front of the French. Anyone else would have knocked the teeth out of all the topmen, but he just says—'come on now, lads'! The old one would have had you flogged and I'd have copped it in the face if he got mad about anything . . . It's a good thing he didn't make us answer for the forty seconds . . .

Several topmen tried to reassure the bo'sun:

—Don't worry, Terentich. We'll do our best!

—He's strict about speed, but he tells us decent . . .

—Encourages, you mean . . . 'Come on, lads'.

—And he didn't rant on and on . . . Don't let me down—and that's the end of it.

—Let's show him what we can do, then!

—Aye, we will!

The loudest and most excited voice was that of the young, red-cheeked topman Nikeyev—the one with big, dark, friendly eyes.

IV

At the very same time the captain was talking in his cabin to his Number One.

—I hope, Vasily Leontich, that we'll show the French up when we furl the sails, and not make a mess of it. Care for a cigar?

—No thank you . . . I'll have a cigarette . . . How did they make a mess of it, Vladimir Nikolaich? Except they set the sails forty seconds later. It's not much of a delay . . .

—It's not much, but it needn't have happened, Vasily Leontich . . . And mustn't happen . . . Our crew are good lads! They don't need floggings . . . One has only to understand the psychology of the Russian sailor . . . Fortunately, I know him!— said Rakitin confidently.

—They're a splendid bunch!—Vasily Leontyevich observed warmly. Then he added guiltily:—Sometimes you hit them . . . habit, you know . . . But if there are grounds for it, they don't mind.

—Still, it would be better if you officers went a bit easier with them . . . Otherwise we might find ourselves mentioned in *The Bell** again . . . Embarassing . . .

The dig was directed at the first lieutenant. He realised this, but said nothing.

—Who was it that could have supplied information about the *Knight*'s former commanding officer? . . Have you read it?

—Yes . . . But I haven't thought who supplied the information.

—It was most likely the distinguished work of junior engineer Nosov. That son of a senior writer calls himself a liberal, you know!—Rakitin said with haughty contempt. He made a wry face and went on:—He preaches rubbish in the wardroom . . . Just an engineer, yet he . . . Don't you let that little engineer get away with too much, Vasily Leontich . . . We are on a warship . . . No question of his engaging in denunciatory literature . . . I can soon get rid of him!—the captain added, emphasising with a particular pleasure his power to 'get rid' of people.

* *The Bell* was a Russian paper published in London by Herzen. In the late 1850s and early 1860s it wielded considerable influence within Russia.

Vasily Leontyevich had very little regard for the 'unscrupulous careerist' he considered Rakitin to be. His demands for fantastic speed, his superciliousness, his boast that he could get rid of an officer, the self-conceit of the man who imagined that he alone had made the *Knight* a model ship, his deviousness and impudence—all filled Vasily Leontyevich with indignation.

'Look at the fop putting on airs and reprimanding me for nothing!'—the first lieutenant thought. He flushed and, restrained by the harsh school of discipline, replied in a dry, official voice:

—Andrey Petrovich Nosov—he deliberately called the engineer by his first name and patronymic—has not said anything provocative in the wardroom which would justify my stopping him. As for what he says in his cabin or on shore, that is no concern of mine. I am a first lieutenant, and not a police spy, sir! If you choose not to permit Andrey Petrovich to write, if indeed he is writing, then please order him accordingly or tell me to convey your order . . .

The brilliant captain valued Vasily Leontyevich as an excellent Number One. He realised his tactlessness and had been taken aback by the words of a man who had seemed a none too clever and pliable veteran. He was all the more vexed because he had not dared to cut his first lieutenant short, when he had so insistently contradicted his captain and refused to carry out an order expressed in the form of advice. Vasily Leontyevich, who had not appeared to want a close relationship with Rakitin from the very first day of his command, now aroused a feeling of malice in the captain's petty, self-centred heart. However, fearing a professional rift, Rakitin showed no sign of displeasure. On the contrary, as though surprised, he said in a most affable, comradely tone of voice:

—Come now, Vasily Leontich! . . Forgive me if I unwittingly offended you . . . I had no thought of reproving you . . . and no reason to . . . A few days ago I was on the bridge and heard the engineer speaking through the open hatch of the wardroom; it seemed to me . . . No doubt you weren't there . . . I am well aware that you would not tolerate anything blameworthy . . . As if I don't know what an ideal and irreplaceable Number One you are, Vasily Leontich!

'What a scoundrel! Totally without principles', thought Vasily Leontyevich. Himself an honest man with principles from which he did not deviate, he yet softened at the captain's flattery and apology.

—I was merely expressing, Vasily Leontich—Rakitin said still more softly and insinuatingly—my opinion of the engineer in a private conversation between friends.

Exhaling fragrant smoke from his expensive cigar, he went on:

—Between you and me, I don't like navigators, engineers and master-gunners . . . They're proper boors . . .

In Rakitin's tone of voice there was profound contempt for those pariahs of the fleet and total certainty that the first lieutenant would be in complete agreement. Though Vasily Leontyevich was not, indeed, devoid of caste prejudice, he was far from feeling the animosity towards corps officers which Rakitin felt, and he said:

—Our navigators, engineer and master-gunner are all worthy officers, Valdmir Nikolaich!

—I wouldn't want them layabouts as well!

—And they're completely decent men . . . If they are not particularly smart . . . not socially refined . . . Well, I don't think that's a defect, Vladimir Nikolaich!

—Very glad to hear such an opinion . . . So ours are a happy exception . . .

Silence ensued.

The first lieutenant got up from his chair and asked:

—You don't require me any longer, Vladimir Nikolaich?

—No, Vasily Leontich.

Vasily Leontyevich left the cabin. Rakitin now loathed his Number One.

V

On the flagship the signal 'Furl sails' had been raised.

The *Knight*'s sailors exceeded even Rakitin's expectations. They were already finishing securing the topsails and topgallants when the French were still moving out along the yards.

—Old women!—said the captain with a cheerful smile and turned his eyes to the *Knight*'s yards.

The sailors, as if by magic, were collecting the soft bulk of the rolled-up topsails and tying them with furling ropes, pressing their feet into the ropes stretched along the yards. They had promised not to let the captain down, and with red, sweating faces were hurrying, like men possessed, for whom every moment was precious. In these seconds they seemed to have lost all sense of self-preservation, to have forgotten that the slender ropes swinging from the moving of their strong, tenacious feet were a dangerous support, requiring careful self-control.

The delighted captain was enjoying the forestaste of victory and just stood admiring his 'lads', as they strained furiously to secure the topsails in accordance with his 'ideal'.

The first lieutenant, on the other hand, felt agitated and was looking aloft anxiously. The sailors' furious haste aroused fears in him, and his conscience was uneasy. So he shouted excitedly:

—Topmen! Careful! Hold on tighter, lads!

Rakitin gave the first lieutenant an angry look, and commented ironically:

—They're not women, Vasily Leontich!

—No, but they are men, Vladimir Nikolaich!—he answered tensely and with meaning.

—I know what they are, sir!—the captain said haughtily, flushing with anger that he was getting a lesson.

No sooner had he said that than before his eyes a man fell off the main-topyard.

Something white struck the rigging, bounced off sideways and hit the deck with a loud thud. There was no cry, no groan.

The sailors working on the quarter-deck gasped and turned away from the motionless man, around whom the deck was already covered with blood. His head was smashed, but Nikeyev's handsome young face was undamaged. His big dark eyes were frozen in a stare of horror.

Many sailors hurriedly crossed themselves. The main-topmen looked down, then started tying the furling ropes once more. But the reckless passion had gone now; the instinct of self-preservation had suddenly appeared.

—Take him to the sick-bay!—the first lieutenant ordered. His voice shook and he did not look at the dead man.

The bo'sun Nikitich had already covered the smashed head, and two quarter-deck men carried Nikeyev below. The sailors averted their eyes, crossed themselves and resumed their work, urged on by the officers. The ship's doctor came running up, pale and alarmed. An old sailor, the brawler and drunkard Kobchikov, who was securing the jib, muttered:

—There's that damned speed for you!

—Silence!—shouted the first lieutenant directing operations on the fo'c'stle.

The work went on apace.

9

—Down from the tops and cross-trees!—Vasily Leontyevich ordered. There was not the former excitement in his voice. He could not get the dead man out of his mind.

The *Knight* was the winner. The sails on the French squadron had still not been furled, while the *Knight* lay with bared masts and secured shrouds.

Despite the Russian corvette's triumph, there was a grim silence on deck. The shaken sailors stood gloomily by their rigging. Only the brawler Kobchikov said quietly to two comrades with an ironic note in his voice hoarse from drink:

—Go on, strain your guts out, says he . . . Snuff it because of a second! . . You're great lads, though! What's it to him that Yegorka has smashed himself to bits . . . Just look at him . . . Different from the Top, who at least has got a heart!

Indeed, the brilliant captain was flushed with his triumph. He tried in vain to look concerned. His still exultant face looked only vexed when he turned to the first lieutenant and said:

—What a careless sailor . . .

Receiving no reply, he asked:

—Who fell off, Vladimir Leontich?

—Yegor Nikeyev . . . It's the second accident now in a month!
—he answered in an agitated and angry tone. Then he gave the order:

—The next watch go below!

The captain was annoyed, raised his head even higher, and went to his cabin. The officers went down to the wardroom, talking among themselves.

Midshipman Lazunsky hurried onto the bridge to begin his watch. Feeling upset and perhaps wishing to share his gloomy thoughts with somebody, he said to the first lieutenant:

—If only you knew what a fine fellow Nikeyev was, Vasily Leontich!

—I did know. I'd be sorry about anyone, any man!—Vasily Leontyevich said in a serious, reflective voice.

—Yes, of course . . . Anyone, Vasily Leontich.

Suddenly blushing, almost with tears in his voice, as though he were afraid that Vasily Leontyevich might think badly of him, he hastened to add diffidently:

—Vasily Leontich, please don't think that I . . . er . . .

—Come now, Boris Alekseich! . . I think . . . I know that you are a fine young midshipman . . . Just stay the same when you are a captain!—he said gently. As he walked away, he added:

—The funeral service will be at eleven . . . Let the captain know at eleven . . . And release half of the watch below.

—Yes, Vasily Leontich!

VI

Half an hour later the first lieutenant made his way to the sick-bay. A crowd was standing at the door, awaiting their turn. The small cabin was full of sailors who had come to look at the dead man and, after crossing themselves, kiss his forehead.

He had already been washed and was lying on a bunk, dressed in clean trousers and shirt, with canvas shoes. His eyes had been closed, and his now yellowish face seemed calm, with that profound and perplexed sort of expression which dead people frequently display. The psalm book was being read at the icon.

Vasily Leontyevich stood there for a minute or two without taking his eyes off the deceased, then made the sign of the cross, bowed to him and went out, experiencing a heavy feeling of guilt.

—Send the bo'sun to my cabin!—he told his orderly.

A minute later Nikitich entered the first lieutenant's cabin.

Vasily Leontyevich ordered the dead man to be brought on deck before the icon and said that there would be two services during the day and that he would be buried in the French cemetery the day after.

—A platoon will attend, and anyone who wants to be there may go.

—Aye-aye, sir.

—One other thing, Kirilov . . . Find out what village Nikeyev came from and whether his parents are alive.

—He has no family alive, sir . . .

—I see. Well, perhaps there's someone close to him back home?

—There is, sir, and for that reason give me leave . . .

—Yes?

—To send Nikeyev's personal effects away. He would say to Ivanov, who's from the same parts, that if he had an accident and fell, he wanted a letter written to Kronstadt and his things sent there without delay . . .

—Very well. I'll send them. What things are there?

—Just a few presents for a woman, sir! A dress, two small

11

rings, a kerchief and forty francs . . . He didn't drink much, sir!

—Right. Bring me them. And give me the address.

—Very grateful, sir . . . He was a nice lad. Open and straight. The whole crew is upset about him . . . A terrific worker he was—and that's why he fell off. He said he wouldn't let the captain down. And he didn't let him down, sir!

—Who am I to send them to? Who is she?

—He was going to marry her properly, once the *Knight* got back. He was saving up presents for her. Yegorka was really daft about that girl—well, not 'girl', sir—that sailor's daughter. And she was daft about him. For three years they were like man and wife . . . She wrote to him a lot . . . She was the only person close to him.

—Tell me, why did a fine lad like Nikeyev think he'd be killed?

—It was just talk, or perhaps he sensed his fate, sir . . . He was on the reckless side. And also the captain told us not to make a mess of things . . . Sort of appealed to us, and Nikeyev got all excited . . . Leave to say one other thing, sir?

—What is it? . . . Speak?

—This speed business, it's wearing the crew out . . . Would you mind asking the captain . . . He's a good man . . . He'll give us a bit of slack, sir . . .

Vasily Leontyevich frowned and promised to speak to the captain.

After the sailor had been buried the first lieutenant cautiously raised the matter with the captain . . . and the upshot of the conversation was that Vasily Leontyevich disembarked the very next day for Russia.

A Terrible
Day

Black, with a shining golden strip running round her, exceptionally elegant and well-proportioned with her three tall masts set slightly back, the four-gun naval clipper *Hawk* was riding solitarily on two anchors on that cold and dreary morning of November 15th, 186– in cheerless Sakhalin Island's deserted Duy bay. The clipper was rocking gently in the swell, dipping her sharp bows in the water and wetting the stays, then lowering her round stern.

The *Hawk* was into the second year of her round-the-world voyage and after visiting the then virtually uninhabited anchorages of our Pacific Maritime Region had called in at Sakhalin in order to lay in free coal mined by the convict deportees recently transferred to the Duy station from the prisons of Siberia. She was then going on to Nagasaki, and from there to San Francisco to join up with the Pacific Squadron.

On that memorable day the weather was wet, with a penetrating sort of chill that made the sailors of the watch huddle in their short pea-jackets and raincoats, while those on the watch below ran frequently to the galley for a warm. There was a fast, fine drizzle and grey mist enveloped the shore. From that direction came only the characteristic, monotonous roar of the breakers over the sand-bars and underwater rocks in the middle of the bay. The wind, while not especially fresh, was blowing straight from the sea, and in the completely exposed roads there was a fair swell which, to everyone's annoyance, impeded quick unloading of the coal from two large, clumsy, antediluvian boats tied to the clipper's side. These were being buffeted and were bobbing about to the alarm of the soldiers aboard them, who'd come from the shore.

With the ceremonial solemnity customary on warships the flag and jack had just been hoisted and from eight o'clock the ship's day began. All the officers, who had come up on deck for the raising of the flag, went down to the wardroom to drink tea.

Only the captain, first lieutenant and the officer of the watch remained upon the bridge, wrapped in raincoats.

—Permission to release the second watch to the bathhouse, sir?—the first lieutenant approached the captain.—The first watch went yesterday . . . The second will be expecting it . . . I've already promised them . . . A bathhouse is something special for sailors.

—Send them, by all means. Only tell them to get back as soon as they can. Once we've loaded we'll be weighing anchor. We'll finish today, I trust?

—We should be finished by four o'clock.

—I'm going at four, anyway —the captain said calmly and authoritatively.—We've hung about long enough in this hole, as it is!—he added, pointing his small, white hand in the direction of the shore.

He pulled the hood of his raincoat from his head, revealing a young, handsome face, full of energy and the calm confidence of a staunch man. He screwed up his mild, sparkling grey eyes slightly and looked intently into the misty distance of the open sea, where the crests of the grey waves showed white. The wind was buffeting his light-brown whiskers and the rain lashed full in his face. For several seconds he did not take his eyes from the sea, as if trying to guess whether it was going to run high. Apparently reassured, he raised his eyes to the overhanging clouds and then listened to the roar of the waves behind the stern.

—Keep an eye on the anchor cable. There's a rotten bottom here, rocky—he said to the officer of the watch.

—Aye-aye, sir!—young lieutenant Chirkov barked cheerfully, raising his hand to the flip of his sou'wester, obviously enjoying the part of an efficient subordinate, his rich baritone voice and real sailor's appearance.

—How much cable has been let out?

—Ten fathoms on both anchors.

The captain made to leave the bridge, but stopped and said once more, turning to the thickset figure of his Number One:

—So see that the longboat returns as soon as possible, Nikolay Nikolaich, will you? The barometer is alright just now, but I'm afraid it might freshen. If there's a head-on wind, the boat won't be able to get back.

—It'll be back by eleven o'clock, Aleksey Petrovich.

—Who'll be going with the crew?

—Midshipman Nyrkov.

—Tell him to get back to the clipper quick, if the weather freshens.

With those words the captain left the bridge and made his way down to his large, comfortable cabin. His nimble orderly took his raincoat at the door, and the captain sat down at a round table, on which coffee and fresh rolls and butter had already been placed.

The first lieutenant, the high priest of the cult of order and cleanliness aboard ship, had as usual been up with the sailors and since five o'clock had been walking about the clipper during the usual morning cleaning. He was now off to snatch a quick glass or two of hot tea before running back on deck to speed up the loading of the coal. When he'd given the watch officer the order to collect the second watch, prepare the longboat and to let him know when the men were ready to go ashore, he hurried down from the bridge and made his way to the wardroom.

Meanwhile the bo'sun Nikitich, or Yegor Mitrich as the sailors respectfully called him, had run up onto the bridge in response to a summons. He put the tar-stained fingers of his strong, toil-hardened hard to the wet cap set back on his head and listened carefully to the watch officer's order.

He was a strong, stocky, stooping, elderly man of the most ferocious appearance: his ugly, pock-marked face was over-grown with hair, he had a rough, short-clipped, bristly moustache, and protruding eyes, like a lobster's, above which black, dishevelled clumps of hair stuck out. His nose, which had long ago been broken by a topsail halyard, put one in mind of a dark-red plum.

However, despite such a ferocious appearance and the foulest swearing with which the bo'sun laced his words to the sailors and his drunken monologues ashore, Yegor Mitrich was the straightest of men; he had a heart of gold, and, moreover, was a bo'sun who knew his job down to the very last detail. He never abused the sailors—neither he nor the sailors, of course, re-garded his swearing as abuse. Though he himself, in his time, had been schooled by beatings, he never knocked anyone about and always spoke up for the men. One need hardly add that he enjoyed the crew's respect and affection.

When he'd heard the watch lieutenant's order the bo'sun hopped off to the fo'c's'le and, taking from his trouser pocket a bronze pipe hanging on a long chain, started an energetic whistling which seemed to presage good news. After he'd finished his whistling with a few trills, displaying the skill of a man who'd spent half of his long navy service blowing a whistle, he bent down over the hatch of the crew's quarters with his short, slightly bow legs well apart and bellowed in a voice somewhat hoarse from his drinking bouts ashore and his swearing:

—Second watch to the bathhouse! Longboat-men to the boat!

After this thunderous shout he ran down the ladder and went round the crew's quarters and orlop-deck repeating the command and scattering choice words of encouragement in the cheeriest tone of voice:

—Look lively, you sons of bitches!.. Turn about like sailors, you devils! Don't dawdle, you bloody clowns!.. You won't get long to steam yourselves . . . You've got to be back on board by eleven . . . Get ready in a second, lads!

Noticing a young sailor who'd still not moved he bawled, trying to make his voice sound angry:

—You, Konopatkin, what are you sitting about for like some bitch of a ma'moiselle, eh? Don't you want to go to the bathhouse, you damned idiot?

—I'm going, Yegor Mitrich, I'm going—the sailor said with a smile.

—Well, collect all your parts, then . . . And don't crawl about like a flea in the damp!—Yegor Mitrich scattered the pearls of his wit to the approving amusement of everyone.

—Will we be leaving here soon, Yegor Mitrich?—asked the clerk.

—Today, I reckon . . .

—Can't be too soon to please me. It's a proper hole. No amusements . . .

—Aye, a hell-hole it is . . . Just the place for poor wretches!.. On with you now, lads!—the bo'sun went on shouting, lacing his shouts with unexpected improvisations.

Pleased that they'd be able to steam in a bathhouse, which they'd not seen for a year and a half, the sailors didn't need the urging of the bo'sun to grab clean underclothes from their canvas bags and provide themselves with soap and pieces of plucked hemp, exchanging remarks the while about the pleasure awaiting them:

—This'll let us remember Mother Russia, any rate. We haven't steamed ourselves since Kronstadt.

—Aye, there's no bathhouses abroad nowhere, just bathrooms. There's brainy people abroad, I'd say, but just fancy—no bathhouses!—an old sailor remarked with a hint of pity for foreigners.

—What, nowhere at all?—asked a young, dark-haired lad.

—Nowhere. The queer lot do without bathhouses. They just have bathrooms everywhere.

—You can keep those damned things!—someone else put in.—I used one in Brest. Say what they like, you can't get a proper wash in one of them.

—Is the bathhouse a good one?

—Aye—replied a sailor who'd been ashore the previous day.—A real hot one. The soldiers built it and knew how to do it too. That bathhouse is just about all they've got here—them and those poor wretches that dig the coal . . .

—Yes, it's a hard life here . . .

—They were saying their commander's a real bastard . . .

—Aye, a proper penal settlement it is! Nowhere to have a drink, no women!

—There's one old woman . . . Our lads saw here . . .

—You'll see her too, don't worry!—Yegor Mitrich said with a laugh.—Beggars can't be choosers! Come on now, come on . . . If you're ready, get out. Cut the cackle, damn you!

The sailors went up one after another carrying bundles under their jackets and lined up on the quarter-deck. The first lieutenant came out and, when he'd repeated to midshipman Nyrkov the order to be back by eleven, told the men to get into the boat which, fitted with masts, was rocking at the port-side.

The sailors climbed cheerfully down the rope ladder, jumped into the sloop and took their seats on the thwarts. Five minutes later the boat, full of men and with raised sails, put off from the side with midshipman Nyrkov at the helm. It sped away with a following wind and had soon disappeared into the misty gloom which still enveloped the shore.

II

In the wardroom everyone was seated at the large table covered with a snow-white tablecloth. Two piles of rolls, made by the officers' cook, butter, lemons, a decanter of brandy, and even cream graced the table—witness to the practical talents and thriftiness of the wardroom treasurer, the young doctor Platon Vasilyevich, who had been elected to that onerous position for the second time. The freshly stoked iron stove allowed them all to sit without coats. They were drinking tea and chatting, mainly cursing Sakhalin whither fate had borne the clipper. They cursed the swell of the roads, the awful weather, the locality, the cold and the slow loading of the coal. For all of them, from the first officer down to the youngest member of the wardroom, the fresh-faced Arefyev, who'd just been promoted to midshipman, the stay in Duy was extremely unpleasant. A shore like this held no attraction for sailors. How could it? A cheerless settlement on a bare, exposed bay with a dreary forest stretching endlessly behind, a few grim-looking barracks in which lived 50 convict exiles, who went out in the mornings to mine coal in a pit that had been sunk nearby, and a half-company of soldiers from a Siberian line-battalion!

When the first lieutenant announced that the *Hawk* would definitely be sailing at four o'clock, even if not all the coal had been on-loaded, everyone expressed delight. The young officers once more began day-dreaming aloud about San Francisco and how they'd 'splash their money around'. Money they certainly had! During those six or seven weeks calling in at various God-forsaken holes of our Far Eastern coastline there had been nowhere to spend money, however much they might have wished to; and now, with another three or four weeks to San Francisco, they'd be able to get rid of three months' pay and get more in advance, if need be . . . After the hellish boredom of all those 'dog-holes' the sailors wanted proper shore-leave. Even such reputable men as the first lieutenant, Nikolay Nikolayevich, who hardly ever went ashore, and if he did, then only for a very short time, to 'refresh himself, as he put it—he, the doctor, the senior gunnery officer, senior mechanic, and even Father Spiridony, were dreaming of the pleasures of a good port, though, naturally, not aloud. They all listened with obvious interest when Snitkin, a plump, cheery lieutenant with chubby lips and small eyes, who was something of a fibber and comic, began telling of the delights of San Francisco, where he'd been on his first round-the-world voyage. With that unrestrained enthusiasm peculiar, it would seem, to sailors, he extolled the beauty and charms of American women.

—Are they really *that* good?—someone asked.

—Magnificent!—Snitkin replied, even kissing his fat fingers

to prove his point.

—Don't you remember praising Malay women, Vasily Vasilich? You reckoned they were good-looking too,—one of the midshipmen observed.

—Well? They're not bad of their type, those dark-skinned girls—Snitkin replied with a chuckle. He was obviously not especially discriminating when it came to the fair sex's colour of skin.—It all depends, old man, on the point of view and the circumstances in which a poor sailor finds himself . . . Ha-ha-ha!

—Your much-vaunted Malay women are bloody awful in any circumstances!

—Well, I declare! What a connoisseur we've got here! All your fine taste didn't stop you falling for that assessor's wife in Kamchatka, did it, though! You kept asking her how to pickle bilberries . . . And the good lady was forty if she was a day, and, more to the point, she was as plain as a pikestaff. Worse than any Malay.

—Oh, I wouldn't say that—the midshipman mumbled in embarassment.

—Say what you like, my friend, a pikestaff she was . . . Why, that wart on her nose was enough in itself . . . Not that it stopped you singing romances . . . So your point of view was pretty clear . . .

—I never did sing—the young midshipman tried to defend himself.

—Remember us sailing from Kamchatka with all that jam, gentlemen?—another midshipman exclaimed.

There was a burst of laughter. They recalled their three-day stop-over in Petropavlovsk on the Kamchatka peninsular. The appearance of the *Hawk* had put all six ladies of the local intelligentsia in a flutter, making them forget their differences for the time being in order to organise a ball for their rare visitors. On the evening of the day they left Kamchatka every one of the clipper's young officers had brought a jar of jam into the wardroom and placed it upon the table with a modest smile of triumph. One can just imagine the initial astonishment and then the amusement when it transpired that all eight jars of jam had been given by one and the same 30-year old lady, who was considered the Kamchatka belle.

—The sly little woman fooled us all!—exclaimed Snitkin.—'This jam is just for you!', says she, and squeezes your hands. Ha-ha-ha! That's pretty good! At any rate she didn't hurt anybody's feelings!

After several glasses of tea and quite a few cigarettes the first lieutenant clearly felt disinclined to leave his place of honour on the soft settee in the warm and comfortable wardroom, especially in view of the animated stories about San Francisco, which reminded this martyr of onerous responsibilities that nothing human was alien to him either. However, being a slave of duty, like most first lieutenants, and one, moreover, who liked to assume the air of a man who doesn't have a moment's rest and has to keep an eye on and answer for everything, he got up decisively (though he couldn't suppress a sour grimace when he remembered what a mess there was on deck), and shouted to the orderly:

—My coat and cape!

—Where are you off to, Nikolay Nikolaich?—asked the doctor.

—That's a strange question, doctor—the first lieutenant replied in an almost vexed tone of voice.—As if you don't know coal is being loaded . . .

So the first lieutenant went on deck to 'inspect' and get wet, though the loading had been proceeding apace without his presence. Nikolay Nikolaich nevertheless still hung around, getting wetter, as though to spite somebody and prove how much he had to endure.

In the wardroom the light-hearted talk continued. The officers had not yet got sick and tired of one another—which happens on very long voyages when there are no fresh impressions from outside. The midshipman kept asking lieutenant Snitkin about San Francisco, and somebody told stories about 'the restless admiral'.* They were all in good cheer.

Only the senior navigator, Lavrenty Ivanovich, took no part in the conversation. He was sucking on his Manila cigar and tapping his bony, wrinkled fingers on the table with no trace of that calm, good-natured look he had when the *Hawk* was on the open sea or riding at anchor in good, protected roads.

He was a lean man of medium height, aged about 50, with an open, agreeable, still fresh-looking face. He was a conscientious, perhaps even over-punctilious veteran, who had long become reconciled to his permanently subordinate position and, unlike most navigators, bore no malice towards commissioned officers.

---

* Admiral Popov, Commander of the Pacific Squadron, see p. xi of Introduction.

Having spent the greater part of his solitary, bachelor life on sea, he had acquired, along with grey hairs and rheumatism, a wealth of experience and toughness of character. He had also acquired a somewhat superstitious, respectfully cautious attitude towards the sea, which had shown him all its many sides during his long voyages.

Obviously worried by something, he left the wardroom and went up onto the bridge. His small, keen eyes, like those of a kite, looked long and hard at the sea and the surroundings. The misty gloom covering the shore had dispersed, and the grey breakers roaring in several parts of the bay at a good distance from the clipper were clearly visible. The old navigator also looked at the swollen pennant, which was showing there was a headwind, and at the leaden sky where small patches of blue were beginning to show through.

—Thank goodness, the rain's stopping, Lavrenty Ivanych— the watch lieutenant Chirkov observed cheerily.

—Aye, it's stopping.

There was no note of satisfaction in the navigator's deep, pleasant voice. On the contrary, he did not seem particularly pleased that the rain was stopping. And as though not trusting his keen eyes, he took the large binoculars from the handrail and peered again into the darkened distance. He examined the clouds hanging above the horizon for several minutes, then replaced the binoculars, sniffed the air like a dog and shook his head thoughtfully.

—Why do you keep on looking, Lavrenty Ivanych? We aren't passing dangerous places, are we?—Chirkov joked.

—I don't like that horizon, sir!—the senior navigator barked.

—Why not?

—In case a wind gets up soon.

—What matter if it does?—the young man said confidently.

—It matters a great deal, sir!!—the navigator observed meaningly.—If that wild north-wester really gets going, it won't let up and we'll not get out of here . . . And I'd rather ride out a storm on the open sea than here, in these damned roads. That's a fact!

—What have we got to be afraid of? We've got an engine. We'll get up steam to help the anchors and ride it out no bother!—Chirkov said confidently.

Lavrenty Ivanovich looked at the young man with the condescending smile of an old, experienced man listening to a boastful child.

—'No bother', you think?—he said with a grin.—Not likely. You don't know what a swine a nor'-wester is, but I do. I was here in a schooner about ten years ago . . . Thank God, we got away in time, otherwise . . .

He didn't finish, fearing, like all superstitious people, even to mention the possibility of disaster. After a short silence he said:

—Alright, we've got an engine, but it's still better to get out to sea while we can! Damn the coal, I say! We can get some in Nagasaki. That sly nor'-wester hits you all of a sudden, and once it's up to storm force, it's too late to leave.

—Come on, Lavrenty Ivanych, you're always seeing danger everywhere.

—When I was your age, I didn't see it either . . . I didn't give two straws, wasn't afraid of anything. But after I'd been in a few nasty scrapes and got a bit older at sea, I knew . . . Well, you know the saying: 'God helps those that help themselves'.

—Why don't you tell the captain?

—What can I tell him? He must know himself what it means to stay here in rough weather!—he answered with some irritation.

Lavrenty Ivanovich, however, did not say that only the day before, on feeling the first breath of a north-west wind, he had spoken to the captain about the 'meanness' of that wind and very cautiously expressed the opinion that it would be better to put to sea. But the proud captain, jealous of his authority, was still enjoying his first years of command and didn't care for anybody's advice. He seemed not to hear the senior navigator's remarks and answered not a word.

—I don't need you to tell me!—his handsome, self-confident face appeared to be saying.

The old navigator had come out of the captain's cabin somewhat put out by such treatment and had muttered once he was on the other side of the door:

—Aye, you're young, aren't you!

—Still, you ought to tell him, Lavrenty Ivanych!—said Chirkov, rather embarassed by the navigator's words, though he tried to hide this by adopting an indifferent tone of voice.

—What's the point of my butting-in with advice? He can see for himself what a lousy place this is!—Lavrenty Ivanovich replied with some annoyance.

At this point the captain came up onto the bridge and began

surveying the horizon, which was completely covered with ominous black clouds. They seemed to be growing and growing, taking up more and more space, then breaking away and climbing up the sky with astonishing speed. The rain had stopped. Around the shore it was brightening.

—The longboat hasn't put off yet?—the captain asked the watch officer.

—No.

—Make the ship's number!

In the captain's usually calm voice there was a barely distinguishable note of anxiety.—The longboat's putting off!—shouted the signaller, who'd been looking at the shore through the telescope.

A strong squally gust of wind suddenly burst into the bay, swept across it, tearing the crests from the waves, and droned in the shrouds. The *Hawk*, which was lying against the wind, withstood it without any bother and simply shuddered on her taut anchor-cables.

—Get up steam, quickly!—said the captain.

The watch officer grabbed the handle of the engine-room telegraph and shouted into the pipe.

—Send the coal boats back to shore! Be ready to weigh anchor!—the captain went on issuing orders in a sharp, authoritative, slightly excited voice, preserving his usual expression of calm confidence.

With his hands in the pockets of his warm coat he began walking up and down the bridge, but stopped every now and again either to peer anxiously into the leaden distance of the roaring sea or to turn and look through the binoculars at the longboat which was making slow progress against the sea-swell and wind.

—You were right after all, Lavrenty Ivanych, and I'm sorry I didn't listen to you and weigh anchor at dawn!—he suddenly announced in what seemed to be a deliberately loud voice, so that both Chirkov and the first lieutenant, who'd hurried up onto the bridge as soon as he'd heard the anchor was to be raised, could hear him.

This confession of error on the part of such a self-confident and proud man who had exhibited courage, coolness and resourcefulness more than once during the voyage completely won Lavrenty Ivanovich over. He suddenly felt embarassed and, as if trying to excuse himself and at the same time justify the captain, he murmured:

—I just mentioned it, Aleksey Petrovich, because I've known what a north-wester can be like here . . . But there's nothing in the manuals.

—It looks as if we're really in for some rough weather!—the captain continued, lowering his voice.—Look!—he added, jerking his head in the direction of the distant clouds.

—It's got the smell of a storm, Aleksey Petrovich . . . My leg's playing up already—the old navigator joked.

—Well, we'll get out to sea while it's working up . . . It can knock us about out there . . .

Again there was a warning gust of wind and the clipper tugged on her chains like a tethered horse.

The captain ordered the topgallant masts to be lowered.

—Be quick with the steam!—he shouted into the pipe.

The topmasts were brought down quickly, and the first lieutenant in charge of the operation smiled with satisfaction at the speed with which it was accomplished. Soon smoke started pouring out of the funnel. The longboat was making better progress. All rowing boats had been raised.

The old navigator was looking more and more anxiously at the threatening clouds covering the horizon. Impatience was to be seen on the captain's face, in his gestures, his voice and in the way he walked. Every so often he would ring down to the engine room and ask about the steam—clearly in a hurry to get out of this bay littered with underwater rocks and poorly charted as well.

Meanwhile, the wind was noticeably freshening. They had to keep slackening the anchor chains because the strong gusts made them as taut as violin strings. With the slacker anchors the clipper moved backwards in the direction of the shore. The swell was increasing, 'white horses' were in evidence, and the *Hawk* was dipping her jib violently.

—Thank God we'll be out of this hole in an hour!—the midshipmen were saying in the wardroom.

—And let's hope we never see it again!

Someone turned to the senior navigator who'd come down to the wardroom for a smoke and a warm.

—Lavrenty Ivanych! When do you reckon we'll get to San Francisco? Will we see those American girls in four weeks, eh?

—No use guessing ahead . . . We're on sea, not ashore.

—Yes, but come on, approximately? . . If everything goes alright.

—What are you keeping on for: when? when? We've got to get out of here first—the navigator said irritably.

—What, is it that rough?

—Go up on deck and take a look!

—We've got a powerful engine, Lavrenty Ivanych. We'll get out.

Lavrenty Ivanovich, who had hardly any doubt that the clipper would not get out before the weather broke and would have to ride it out in the roads, made no answer. Full of the gloomiest thoughts about the clipper's situation in the event of a real storm, he took quick, nervous draws on what remained of his cigar.

At this point young midshipman Nyrkov burst into the wardroom. Drenched and red with cold, he exclaimed in a cheerful, excited voice:

—It's a hell of a wind, gentlemen, I can tell you. It got so rough half way back that I thought we wouldn't make it . . . We all got drenched to the skin . . . And the cold . . . I'm frozen. Hey, orderlies! Let's have some hot tea and brandy quick!—he shouted and went off to his cabin to change, happy that he'd got back safely and by eleven o'clock. Still a very young sailor on his first long cruise, he had naturally been too ashamed to say how terrified he had felt in the longboat lashed by the waves, and how he had tried with a casual air to encourage the weary, sweating oarsmen, promising them three tots per man.

—Well, no point in waiting now . . . Get up steam and off to the American girls . . . What do you say, Lavrenty Ivanych?—said the cheery lieutenant Snitkin with a laugh.

Lavrenty Ivanovich, however, merely gave a shrug, put on his old service cap and went up on deck.

III

The old navigator's fears were well-founded. Hardly had the longboat been raised to the booms and secured when, after three fierce, consecutive gusts of wind, the storm broke—one of those storms that alarm even old, experienced seamen.

Ragged black clouds were racing across the sky, where small patches of blue were barely showing through now, and were covering the whole horizon. Although it was morning, it was as dark as at dusk. The sea was boiling. Huge waves were overtaking one another, and as they crashed noisily together, scattered a diamond spray which was caught up by the wind and borne further. The terrible roar of the violent sea merged with that of the diabolical wind. Meeting an obstacle in the clipper, it either howled angrily or moaned piteously in the rigging, hatches and muzzles of the guns, bent the topmasts, shook the boats on the davits, tore away all objects not lashed down and pulled at the innumerable shrouds.

Like a mad, infuriated beast, it threw itself on the little clipper, threatening to destroy her and all on board her. And the *Hawk*, meeting her enemy head-on, would keep shuddering on her moorings, so that it seemed that at any moment she might be torn from her taut, droning chains. The poor ship was being pulled about on them more and more, she was squeaking in all her timbers, as though from pain, and was pitching furiously. Her jib would plunge into the water and when she rose, she would shake the water off, like some gigantic bird.

The captain was standing on the bridge with his cap pulled down tight over his forehead and keeping firm hold of the rail with one hand. In the other hand he held a loudspeaker. The icy wind was blowing full in his face, piercing him with cold, but the captain, who had already been on the bridge for about an hour, seemed not to feel the wind; he was terribly serious and pre-occupied, yet apparently completely calm. However, this calm cost him some effort and was only the outer calm of a sailor able to control himself at moments of crisis. His heart was racked with anxiety, his whole being was experiencing that nervous strain which, if repeated frequently, can age sailors prematurely and make them grey before their time. He well appreciated the danger of the clipper's position and that of the men entrusted to him, and, in view of his terrible responsibility, was feeling bitter pangs of conscience. His presumption was certainly to blame for everything . . . Why had he not heeded the advice of the navigator yesterday? Why had he not put to sea? . . Whereas now . . .

Where's the steam?!—he shouted, jerking the handle of the engine-room telegraph.

The engine-room answered that it would take another ten minutes.

Ten minutes in a hellish storm like this, which was threatening to tear the clipper from her anchors at any moment, was like an eternity! With the engine working to help the anchors one might still hold fast and ride it out . . . And so the captain, who was usually restrained and did not resort to abuse, and who knew very well that they couldn't get up steam any quicker, neverthe-less swore at the engine-room through the communication pipe, making the senior engineer, who was straining every nerve as it was, go as pale as a sheet and clench his fists convulsively.

The captain was no longer peering ahead into the open sea, on whose broad expanse he would so like to have been at that moment, with the *Hawk* under storm sails and with battened-down hatches, scudding over the waves like a corked barrel until the storm passed. He turned round frequently to look anxiously in the direction of the shore—to where amid the raging sea, just to the left of the settlement, a grey line of foam from breakers on a long reef was clearly visible like a broad, winding ribbon. This submerged reef, which so troubled the captain despite its distance, lay exactly facing the sea, in the very heart of the roads exposed to the north-wester. On the other two sides stretched a precipitous shore, near which reef-waves were also crashing in places. Only to the left was there a tiny inlet washing the mouth of a narrow valley, which seemed to be free of underwater rocks.

—Is the sheet-anchor ready?—the captain asked the first lieutenant after he'd reported that the decks and hold had been checked and that everything was in order: the guns had been secured and everything lashed down.

—It's ready.

—The chains are all let out?

—All let out and all stretched taut, Aleksey Petrovich—I'm just praying they don't break and we don't lose the anchors—the first lieutenant said gloomily.

The captain was worrying about that very thing, and here was his Number One reminding him! Clearly trying to restrain himself, he said impatiently:

—We'll worry about that, if it happens, Nikolay Nikolaich. It's early yet!—And added:—See that the pumps are in working order, will you!

—Aye-aye, sir!—answered the first lieutenant, somewhat offended because he thought the captain did not sufficiently appreciate his constant 'hard labour', and left the bridge to inspect the pumps personally, hardly thinking in his professional solicitude what they might be needed for.

Now that the danger he had feared had come, the senior navigator was standing by the compass with a fatalistic sort of calm. He had his hands in the pockets of his short overcoat and had planted his 'sea-legs' wide apart on the violently pitching bridge. Apparently this terrible storm with its possible results did not especially frighten Lavrenty Ivanovich, who had been face to face with death more than once. His stance, his resolute and composed face, his steady, reflective grey eyes looking at the breakers all seemed to be saying: 'What will be will be!'

Lieutenant Chirkov, despite the dashingly casual air he was trying to assume, was obviously scared stiff. He was pale, and with every shudder the clipper gave he surreptitiously crossed himself and shouted in an agitated voice:

—Foredeck! Watch the cable!

Almost all the officers had come up on deck from the comfortable wardroom and were looking at the hell around them with strained faces. There was no question of getting out to sea, and no one could say how long this accursed storm would rage.

Five minutes passed—unusually long ones for the captain. The steam would be ready anytime now and the agonising anxiety would be over. The *Hawk*, despite the intensifying storm, was still holding fast on her anchors and not drifting.

But just as the captain was thinking this very thought, the clipper gave an unusually violent shudder and lurched backwards as a sharp clang came from the foredeck. The bo'sun Yegor Mitrich rushed headlong to the quarter-deck and roared:

—The chains have snapped!

As though happy to be free of the chains the *Hawk* veered to the side and was driven backwards by the wind.

The sheet-anchor was quickly shot and checked the clipper for a minute. Then, as if cut by a knife, this chain snapped as well.

—Full steam ahead! Steer to port!—the suddenly pale captain ordered in a loud, firm voice.

Thank God! The engine started up and the screw propellor began turning behind the stern. The clipper was stopped in her dangerous course and put against the wind.

The captain's serious face brightened. But not for long.

Despite the engine's intensive efforts, the clipper could barely hold her position against that cruel wind. The storm was getting stronger, and the *Hawk* began to drift noticeably backwards.

—Maximum steam ahead!

The engine's pulse increased even more, but could the *Hawk* withstand such a hurricane?

Suddenly the stern gave a shudder, as if it had touched some obstacle. The screw stopped turning, broken the moment the stern had swung round against what must have been a rock.

Now, quite helpless, without propellor, without anchors, no longer obeying the helm, lying adrift the turbulent sea, the clipper was borne rapidly towards a long line of rocks, marked by the grey spray of waves breaking at no great distance.

IV

A cry of horror broke from a hundred throats and froze on distorted faces and in wide-open eyes staring at that white, seemingly inflated ribbon of water in the distance. They were all immediately aware of the inevitability of destruction, that only some ten minutes separated them from certain death. There could be no doubt that the clipper would be smashed to pieces on that long line of rocks towards which the storm was driving her with terrifying speed, and there was no hope of escape amid those tempestuous waters. At this thought they were gripped by the anguish of despair, reflected in the convulsive twitching of their deathly pale faces, their stilled eyes and involuntary sighs.

Death itself seemed now to be looking upon that handful of sailors with impassive cruelty from those roaring, towering, leaden waves which breathed an icy coldness. They were raging all around, shaking the poor ship, throwing her from side to side like a chip of wood, their crests crashing down on the deck in showers of icy spray.

The sailors were taking off their caps, crossing themselves and murmuring prayers through pale lips. On some faces there were tears, while others wore an expression of unusually stern seriousness. One very young sailor, Oparkov, a cheery, good-natured lad who'd been sent on a world cruise straight from the plough and was terrified of the sea, suddenly gave out a loud moan, followed by a burst of insane laughter and, waving his arms about in all directions, ran to the ship's side, jumped onto the rigging, and with the same hollow laugh threw himself into the sea, where he immediately disappeared in the waves.

Another equally young sailor, crazed with despair, tried to follow his example; with a wild wail he too made for the side, but the bo'sun Yegor Mitrich caught him by the neck and cursed him for all he was worth. This cursing brought the man to his senses. He moved sheepishly back from the ship's side, slowly making the sign of the cross and weeping like a child.

29

Some old sailors, observing tradition, came down onto the orlop-deck, hurriedly put on clean shirts and went to the large icon of St. Nicholas the Miracle-Worker, which was fixed there. When they'd kissed it and prayed, they went back on top to die with the others.

Despite all the horror of the situation there was not the panic among the crew, which usually seizes men at such moments. They were held back by the habit of strict navy discipline and by the presence on the bridge of the captain, first lieutenant, officer of the watch and senior navigator, who remained at their posts as though the clipper was not speeding to destruction. Like frightened sheep the sailors pressed together in a crowd by the mainmast, their eyes moving with piteous resignation from the sea to the bridge and back.

The officers were standing on the quarter-deck and under the bridge. Stout lieutenant Snitkin, recently so cheery, was shaking all over as if in fever, hardly able to keep on his feet from the terror that gripped him. He was hurriedly crossing himself, looking mournfully and distractedly at the others and, as though ashamed of his faintheartedness, was trying to smile—but instead of a smile there appeared a sort of martyred grimace. The doctor, Platon Vasilevich, kept screwing up his eyes, as if they were hurting him, and would then peer intently at the sea again. On his amiable, intelligent face was an expression of almost infinite sorrow. He kept thinking of his young wife whom he loved so much, regretting bitterly, now it was too late, that he'd come on this voyage instead of retiring. Without realising it, he kept saying aloud: 'Why? . . Why? . . Why? . .'—and screwed up his eyes again. Nyrkov, who'd been so glad to have escaped drowning in the longboat, was trying to hide his terror at the approach of certain death. The shame of revealing it before the fearless captain (so it seemed to him), the officers and crew made this fine young midshipman force himself to seem calm and ready to die 'in a manner befitting a good sailor'. But all the time his heart was faint with anguish and he felt cold shivers running down his spine. 'Shame, shame!'—he thought, raising his dark eyes in silent, hopeless entreaty to the heavens covered with racing, dark storm clouds. But in them he saw the same face of death hovering over the clipper. The master gunner and engineer, both elderly men, when they'd run up on deck and seen the situation the clipper was in, rushed to their cabins and began stuffing money and valuables into their pockets. They both had families in Kronstadt. Both had denied themselves everything, rarely going ashore so as not to spend money. When they'd filled their pockets, they went back up on deck and only then, it seemed, did they realise that they'd not be able to save anything, that their families would be orphaned. They looked around with terror in their eyes, mechanically clutching their pockets at the same time. Father Spiridony, fat, round, and smooth as a cat, had fed himself well at the plentiful wardroom table after his meagre monastic fare; now, with his cassock flying in the wind, he was clinging to one of the posts supporting the bridge and repeating prayers uncomprehendingly, his jaws trembling and his large, round eyes bulging with terror.

The officers on the quarter-deck and the sailors crowded round the mainmast kept looking up at the captain. Their eyes were saying:

—Save us!

V

Like a cornered wolf, pale and angry, yet still retaining his self-control, the captain seemed to be rooted to the bridge, searching with hungry, burning eyes for a way of saving his men and his ship. He seemed to be aware of those entreating, reproachful looks, and the thought that he was to blame for this disaster flashed through his mind again, making the muscles of his tense face contract. There appeared to be no way out. Not more than a minute had passed since the clipper had started moving towards the reef, but that minute had been like an eternity. Another ten minutes to so, and the clipper would hit the rocks, and that would be the end of them all . . .

Suddenly his eyes fastened on a small inlet to starboard and a flash of joy lit up his face. He immediately shouted into the loudspeaker in a confident, authoritative voice:

—Set the sails! Topmen to the shrouds! Quick now! Every second counts, lads!

The confident voice awakened in everyone a vague kind of hope, though no one as yet understood why the sails were being set.

The old navigator gave a start and looked at the captain with a mixture of surprise and admiration. Guessing what was up, he began looking through the binoculars at the same inlet, which was almost hidden by high banks.

—I'm going to beach her!—the captain said in a sharp, excited voice, turning to his Number One and the navigator.—It seems clear there . . . No rocks, are there?—he added, pointing to the inlet with a chilled, ham-red hand.

—Shouldn't be!—the navigator answered.

—What about the depth by the shore?

—Three and a half fathoms, according to the chart.

—Excellent. We'll be there in no time under half-wind.

—Let's just hope the masts don't snap!—put in the first lieutenant.

—A fine time to be talking like that!—the captain said casually. He raised his head and shouted into the loudspeaker: —Quick now, lads, quick!

But the 'lads', swaying violently on the yards and gripping the crosspieces tightly with their feet, needed no encouragement in their haste to release the topsails and reefs, despite the hellish wind threatening to tear them at any moment from the yards into the sea or onto the deck. Holding onto the yard with one arm and pressing himself into it, every topman was doing his devilishly difficult job with his free hand at a terrifying height in an icy blizzard. They had to hold onto the bulky sails with their teeth and tore their nails till they bled.

Finally, after about eight minutes, during which the clipper had drawn so near the breakers that the black-looming rocks could be glimpsed with the naked eye, the sails were set, and the *Hawk*, with topsails under four reefs, leaped to the wind again, like an obedient, well-bridled horse. Lying over, almost touching the waves with her side, she now sped towards the shore, leaving the terrible, foaming ribbons of breakers behind her to port.

They all crossed themselves. Hope of deliverance showed on every face. The bo'sun was swearing again with his usual energy for a slack staysail-sheet and looking anxiously up at the bending masts.

—Save your chronometer, Lavrenty Ivanych!—said the captain, when the clipper was near the shore.—We'll take a hell of a bump when we beach.

The clipper was flying like a seagull under a following wind straight at shore. There was a hushed silence on deck.

—Hold tight, lads!—the captain shouted, gripping the rail. Release the fore-topsail stays! Away with the staysail!

The sails fluttered, and the *Hawk* skimmed into the inlet at speed, cutting deeply into the soft, sandy bottom.

VI

—Thanks, lads, you did a fine job!—the captain said, going round the ship's company.

—Thank you, sir!—the sailors answered happily. And some said:—God bless you!

The captain ordered two lots of vodka to be distributed and a hot meal prepared as soon as possible. Then he went down with the first lieutenant to inspect the damage to the clipper. There turned out to be not all that much damage, and there was almost no water in the hold. Only the beaching had damaged the engine and displaced the galley.

—The *Hawk* is a good ship, Nikolay Nikolaich.

—A fine shipe!—the first lieutenant answered with real affection.

—Let the men rest up today . . . It's a good place to be . . . The storm won't bother us—the captain continued.—Tomorrow we'll start lightening the ship bit by bit, off-load the supplies, and haul the clipper a bit further ashore so as to winter here more securely and not worry about the ice . . .

—Aye-aye, sir!

—Have we enough supplies to last us till spring?

—Enough for six months.

—We'll spent a decent enough winter in this hole, then—the captain observed as he came up from the engine-room.

Happy, frozen, and terribly hungry, the officers went down to the wardroom and hurried the orderlies to serve vodka and a bite to eat, and to get the stove going. There was no question yet of dinner. Everything that had been prepared in the morning had been spoiled in the dislocated galley.

—So much for San Francisco!—said lieutenant Snitkin after a few minutes' relieved silence. He had got over his terror and was feeling rather embarassed that he had shown his faint-hearted despair.

—Just thank the Lord that the fish aren't eating you!—Lavrenty Ivanovich observed in a serious voice, downing a copious measure of rum, which he followed with a mouthful of Cheshire cheese.—But for our good captain we'd be at the bottom of the sea now. He got us out of it . . . What a sailor!

And the old navigator downed another.

They all expressed agreement with these words, and then the door opened. There was silence. The captain and first lieutenant came in.

—Well, gentlemen—the captain said, taking off his cap—we'll be wintering here in this dump, rather than in San Francisco . . . We've no choice! I wouldn't listen to Lavrenty Ivanych yesterday . . . Now we shan't get away before the spring . . . I'll let the Squadron Commander know at the first opportunity, and he'll send a ship for us. It'll take us to dock to get repaired and we'll sail on the *Hawk* again . . . Say, why are you all looking at me like that?—he added suddenly, noticing the astonished looks directed at his head.

—You've gone grey, Aleksey Petrovich!—the old navigator said quietly, with affectionate respect.

Indeed, his fair head was almost grey.

—Gone grey?! Well, that's not much—the captain said.—It could have been a great deal worse . . . Well, gentlemen, what do you say? Can I have a bit to eat with you? I'm starving.

They were all delighted to seat him on the sofa.

*

In the spring the 'restless admiral' himself came for the clipper on the corvette *Eager* and officially expressed thanks to the captain for the resourcefulness and courage 'with which at a critical juncture he had saved the crew and ship entrusted to his care'. A few days later the *Hawk* was towed into Hong Kong, where she was repaired. A month later, slim, trim and elegant as before, she set sail for the shores of Australia.

Issy

I

Not only the officers but all the sailors called this small, pale, frail-looking man with a typically Jewish hooked nose, thin lips, and large, dark eyes not by his surname, as is usual, but by the familiar form of his first name, Isaak—Issy. He was never called anything else, though he was gone forty and was an old sailor who had served 16 of the then obligatory 25 years in the navy as a sailmaker.

He had long become used to this name. He had received it after he had appeared at a recruiting office opened in one of the towns of the North-Western Region. There, pale as death, thin as a matchstick, in a soiled, torn, long-tailed coat and with sidelocks, he had heard, despite his narrow chest on which he had placed such hope, the fateful word: 'Forehead'.* Despite his mother's sobs and his father's prostrations before the military doctor, he was shaven. For some reason (probably because of his height) he was assigned to the navy and shortly afterwards was sent with a party of recruits to Kronstadt. From the very first day the men in the naval depot began calling him Issy. And Issy he remained all his days.

—The name doesn't matter. What matters is not being beaten or getting the lash!—Issy reasoned and was not in the least offended that he was not called like Russians, particularly as the sailors' attitude towards him was very good, not devoid even of a certain esteem. Absolutely everyone, not excepting bo'suns and petty officers, respected Issy as a wholly decent man—honest, quiet, hard-working, and 'brainy' as well, a man who on occasion could explain what no one else could. According to the sailors there was 'nothing beyond' Issy. He could speak so eloquently and persuasively that he was listened to with pleasure,

---

* Until 1874 men recruited into the Russian navy or army had the front part of the head shaven.

despite his Jewish accent. When he had entered the navy he had taught himself to read and write, and read not just Jewish books but Russian ones too. He liked to occupy himself with a book, which in those days was very rare among sailors, the vast majority of whom were illiterate, and he readily talked about what he'd read. And this gave him the authority of a 'learned man', which he ably exploited.

Issy's reputation was long established among the crew with whom he'd served from the day he'd become a sailor, and this deserved reputation was not tarnished in any way.

True, some sailors held that, though Issy was a good man, he was still a 'yid' after all, and was to some extent to blame for Judas's having betrayed the Saviour for 30 pieces of silver and that Issy's forefathers, admittedly distant ones, had crucified Christ. However, Issy's personal qualities—he was not capable of harming so much as a fly, let alone betraying or crucifying anybody—largely mitigated his guilt for the crucifixion even in the eyes of the rabid anti-Semites, among whom the stout, ginger-haired clerk Avdeyev stood out particularly with his categorical opinions and the utterly incredible things he told about Jews. Even he, however, was finally obliged to agree that Issy was not at all like a 'dirty Jew' and would not stoop to 'their dirty tricks'. What mainly convinced him was the fact that Issy was not greedy for money. Avdeyev knew this particularly well; for three years he had not repaid three roubles he'd borrowed from Issy, taking advantage of his tactfulness. And the clerk sometimes expressed regret that Issy would not adopt Christianity.

—Then he'd be a really decent person!—he would add.

Others had also talked to Issy about this before.

Father Spiridony, the deep-voiced monk* from Valaamsky Monastery, who had served as priest on the ship for several voyages and whose cassock Issy had cleaned and thoroughly repaired on several occasions after Father Spiridony had been ashore, had once started a conversation on that ticklish subject.

—I must say you're a very good, unmercenary man, Issy.— Father Spiridony said in his deep voice, which was rather hoarse after being 'ashore', as he took his cassock from Issy.—For example, you mend the clothes of a servant of God, who is of a completely different faith, and demand no reward for so doing.

---

*In those far-off days at the beginning of the 'thirties poorly educated monks, who had not completed their training anywhere, were appointed to ships of the fleet to perform religious duties. Subsequently selection was more careful. (Author's note.)

Does that not show truly Christian virtue in you, Issy? . . Another man, a Christian even, would take 10 kopecks from a priest, and here are you, a Jew devoid of God's grace, and you don't take anything—he went on, extremely pleased that Issy never so much as hinted about a reward for his work.—And I know that in the future, if I need to have recourse to your services, you'll not refuse. Isn't that so, Issy?

Issy replied that he'd always be glad to be of service, if there were anything to mend.

—That's just my point . . . I'm saying that you have a Christian soul, even if your faith, to put it bluntly, is false. And don't you go and get angry at the truth, Issy—everybody thinks it's false!—Father Spiridony insisted, wearing a good-natured, cheerful smile on his full, slightly swollen face.

Issy made no objection, but obviously not wishing to continue the conversation in that direction, he asked cautiously and respectfully:

—So you don't need anything else just now, Father?

—No, you just wait, Issy. I've got something to say to you.

—You speak and I'll listen,—Issy replied tactfully, slightly inclining his head on which curls were beginning to appear.

—You know what, Issy? Give up your Jewish faith, be done with it. Accept God's grace and become a member of the true Christian church. The thing is—I feel sorry for you, Issy . . . you're such a good-living man and yet your soul is on the road to hell. Believe what I'm saying: on the road to hell! Where do you think the Jews' place in the next world is, eh? In Gehenna, the fiery furnace. And what is preordained for them? What do you think?

—You'd know best,—Issy murmured diplomatically.

—Swallowing burning coals!—Father Spiridony explained categorically and added:—Best be converted . . .

—What can I do! If merciful God is so angry at the Jews, like you say, that He has ordained that they swallow burning coals, then I'll swallow burning coals, if there are enough to go round, but I won't change my faith. I was born into my faith, and in that faith I'll die, Father—Issy answered. And turning his hat in his hands, he again asked:

—So, with your permission, I'll leave, if you don't need anything else?

—You're a foolish man, Issy, if you don't want to save your soul.

—I clearly am foolish—Issy agreed, a slight, barely noticeable smile flitting across his face.—But perhaps you need something else repaired?

—No thanks, Issy. Everything is alright just now . . . I see that you're deaf to the truth. You just think about what I've said.

—Why not think about it? We must think about everything—that's what God gave man reason for. And He didn't leave out the Jew!—Issy added with a barely perceptible note of irony and slipped out of the cabin.

—He'll not heed me!—Father Spiridony thought with a sigh. And when he'd admired his superbly repaired lustrine cassock, he felt sorry a good Jew like Issy would be bound to have a hard time in the next world.

II

There was another, more serious attempt on Issy's soul on the part of the elderly wife of an admiral in Kronstadt. In the autumn of her years, after a merry life which had little in common with her recently-acquired views on feminine virtue and conjugal duty she now lavished her still abundant store of emotion not upon earthly but spiritual conquests.

Issy was making boots for the admiral's wife (he was a skilled and stylish shoemaker), receiving for his labour whatever she 'cared to give'. Taking advantage of the fact that Issy was a navy employee and had been sent to her by a naval commander subordinate to her husband, the good lady 'cared to give' unconscionably little, but was quite willing to save Issy's soul by turning him onto the path of truth.

So one day, after she'd handed Issy a 20-kopeck piece for the most elegant boots with French heels and had given him a gracious nod in answer to his: 'Most obliged, your ladyship!', she took a few steps to see if the boots fitted nicely and, well pleased, sat herself in an armchair with the words:

—You're a Jew, aren't you, Issy?

—Yes, your ladyship!—Issy replied, stepping back to the door.

The admiral's wife gave a sigh and started speaking about lost souls. She spoke with some fervour about truth and spiritual rebirth, darkness and light, clearly enjoying her own eloquence, and finished by advising Issy to change his religion, promising him certain material benefits besides the salvation of his soul.

She knew that Issy was a good, honest man, and would ask her husband for him to be made a petty officer and left on shore.

The proposal was a tempting one, especially the prospect of being permanently on dry land, which Issy had always considered incomparably more pleasant and convenient than the high seas. Standing stiffly at attention with his hands along the seams of his trousers, he had listened to her spiritual exhortation with such apparently rapt attention that she had virtually no doubt of saving him. Her once beautiful eyes surveyed him with favour. She shook two grey curls decorating her faded cheeks and said solemnly:

—Naturally you do want to be a Christian, Issy, don't you? I'll be your godmother!—she added with a gracious smile.

Well-mannered himself and appreciating good manners in others, and anyway by nature a very gentle man, Issy summoned to his aid all his diplomatic skill and resourcefulness so as not to offend the lady and provoke her displeasure by rejecting her kind proposal in any way that might appear disrespectful. And, truth to tell, he was also afraid that some serious trouble might befall him. Who knew what his superiors might think? His heart sank at the very thought.

He began by making several low bows and expressing his thanks that such a high-placed lady should deign to bestow her gracious attention on such an unworthy person as himself. Could he have hoped for such an honour? And he continued bowing and expressing thanks in the most refined language he could think of, but he didn't answer the lady's question and even ventured to pass quite skilfully from expressions of gratitude to the offer of making summer shoes for her in the latest foreign style, like the ones the wife of Admiral Gvozdyov had brought back from Paris.

—I saw those shoes at her house . . . Oh, such style, your ladyship, how perfectly put together!—he enthused.—And they'll only cost you two roubles with my material!—he added, deciding to put one and a half roubles of his own towards them just to please the stingy lady and deflect her attention from his soul.

She graciously accepted the offer and enquired about the shoes in some detail. Issy was on the point of finally taking his leave, having promised to work on the shoes and bring them in five days time, when she asked:

—Why haven't you answered my question, Issy? Do you want to be baptised?

Issy suddenly adopted a serious and secretive expression and, lowering his voice, said somewhat confidentially:

—I daren't, your ladyship.

—Why not?

—Because of my father and mother, your ladyship. I feel sorry for them.

—Why on earth are you sorry for them?

—Your ladyship, they're old, foolish people, they live in the back of beyond, and in their ignorance would say: 'How can you change your religion like a nightshirt?'—pardon the expression, your ladyship, and they'd think that their son Issy had sold his conscience and acted like the lowest of men. My father and mother don't know a lot, your ladyship, they don't know which religion is the most correct, and would ask: 'How is it, Issy, that Russians don't change their religion but live by the one into which they were born, while you, Issy, have changed yours, eh?' And they'd say: 'Curse you for it, Issy!' And they'd go on weeping that they had a son like me and would die of broken hearts, your ladyship! I'd feel very ashamed and hurt if my father and mother died because of me. Terribly ashamed! But God grant your ladyship happiness and health for your gracious concern for my sinful soul . . . And your husband and children too . . . Perhaps you'd like me to make boots for them?—he added unexpectedly and began bowing again.

His clever reference to his father and mother, who had long been resting peacefully in their graves, the argument which he'd put into those 'foolish' people's mouths, and, finally, the truly fabulous cheapness of the shoes he'd promised—all these things made a favourable impression on the lady, and in view of Issy's difficult position she no longer insisted on saving his soul, but even praised him for his love and respect for his parents.

—The children don't need new boots just yet, Issy. The ones they have are still good.

Feeling very relieved, even cheered, Issy sententiously observed that 'every man should respect his parents', and added:

—So you'd like buckles on the shoes, your ladyship?

—Wouldn't bows be better, Issy?

—As you wish, your ladyship, only, if I may say so, buckles would be stronger . . . Of course you could have bows, but the latest fashion is buckles, and Admiral Gvozdyov's wife has buckles on her shoes.

—Well, put buckles on mine too, then.

—Yes, your ladyship.

Issy was in no hurry to leave now, for he was sure the awkward conversation was over. Noticing the lady's good mood, he conceived a bold idea—to take advantage of it so that through her he might get out of sailing and fix himself up on shore without risking his soul. So, shifting carefully from one foot to the other, he said:

—I'll try to make your shoes just as good as the foreign ones, your ladyship. And whatever you want to order for yourself and the young masters I'll make top quality. Only I won't be able to in the summer because I'll be sent to sea . . . It's in the summer that the young masters' shoes have most wear,—he emphasised—and I'm not around . . . If I were on shore, your ladyship, I could repair them and make new ones . . . You'd only have to say.

—Right, I'll tell my husband—she declared.

—I'm most grateful! Keep well, your ladyship!—replied the overjoyed Issy and, turning round by the left as etiquette demanded, he went out.

Issy, however, did not remain ashore but was sent to sea that same summer. The admiral's wife forgot her promise and soon moved with her husband to Petersburg. Issy had no one to ask. Moreover, he was greatly valued on the ship as an excellent sailmaker.

Still, with her ladyship's departure there were no further attempts by anyone to save his soul and, firm in his religion, he piously carried out, as far as he was able, all the observances it prescribed. Every Friday evening, whether he was on shore or at sea, he would find some secluded corner, put on his prayer shawl and pray fervently, singing his monotonous chants in a quiet, nasal voice. As such times his pale, thin face with large, dark eyes was lit up with exaltation and a kind of gentle sorrow, and his voice trembled from a flood of religious feeling.

And never did any sailor allow himself a sneer or insulting remark. Far from it! They would all pass carefully by the Jew standing at prayer, and many, marvelling at his fervour, would say quietly, wonderingly:

—A Jew, and so mindful of his God!

III

Issy was never reproached either for his fear of the sea, especially when it began to get rough, or for a sort of unsurmountable, purely physical dread of risk and the dangers associated with a sailor's life.

Issy really could not overcome this feeling in himself and, of course, he had never made a real sailor. His 16 years in the service he had spent as a 'non-combatant' sailmaker. Not once had he been able to climb to the top—his courage had always failed him and, after crossing a few shrouds, he had come down. He felt infinitely happier on the deck and no longer ventured to repeat the voluntary attempts he'd made at the beginning of his service, since his non-combatant status exempted him from specifically sailors' tasks. Only during emergencies, when all hands were called, did he have to serve 'on deck': to help to haul a rope, stand by the capstan when the anchor was raised, and so on—tasks which he always performed with remarkable zeal. He would haul conscientiously on the rope or bear down with his chest upon the capstan-arm, using all his meagre strength, eager and proud to show that he too could work as hard as others.

But everything on the ship that was higher than the deck frightened him and he would look with awe at the tops of the tall masts. The mere thought that he might suddenly be sent in rough weather to furl the topsail, standing on a rope stay of the furiously swaying yard-arm, or onto the jib-boom ploughing into the sea to take in the jib-sails made him go cold all over. He would screw up his eyes and, as if to ward off some terrible spectre, would helplessly extend his small, thin hands—hands that weren't like those of a sailor but had slender, bony fingers which worked superbly with the enormous sail needle.

—The Lord made Issy the way he is, and he's not to blame. He'd be glad to do it, but he can't. His stomach just won't take it. If you sent him to the topgallant yard, he'd die of fright!'

—He wouldn't get that far, he'd fall into the sea.

—He's just not cut out to be a sailor.

—Aye, and he's as weak as a sparrow.

That was the way the sailors talked about him. While they were ready to criticise and grin at any sign of cowardice in their comrades, in their talk about Issy they used a special measure. If some old sailor would occasionally have a laugh at him, it was good-natured and there was never any intention to denigrate or offend him, the more so as Issy himself made no attempt to conceal his weakness.

—God gave me most things—reason, willingness to try, patience—but He didn't give me a sailor's courage, lads . . .

Obviously, every man has his apportioned lot, and God didn't want the Jew to be a sailor . . . 'Be a workman and live on dry land'—that's what God ordered the Jew—he would add, ascribing to the Lord God his own cherished desires.

—Issy, what if the first lieutenant sent you to the yard-arm for a spell!—one of the petty officers or old sailors joked.

—He wouldn't send me! Why should he?

—As a punishment.

—Go on! What would he punish me for? I mend the sails and nobody sees me. I do my job well . . . The first lieutenant is a sensible man . . .

—Sensible he may be, but if he got his dander up, he wouldn't think . . . There's a lot you can pick on for no reason . . . You can't be sure. He'd see you on deck and shout: 'Send Issy to the yard-arm. Let him get some ventilation!'

In Issy's exceptionally vivid imagination—he well knew what unforeseen things happened on a warship—the idea of the possibility of something of the sort instantly formed into a clear picture. He exclaimed in alarm:

—O–oh! It couldn't happen!

Then he realised just as quickly that it was nonsense, that they were playing with him, and, smiling, he said good-naturedly:

—Don't you go scaring me, Matveich. I get scared enough as it is.

In rough weather he usually felt poorly and ill-at-ease, though he wasn't sea-sick. On occasions when the great wooden ship was being beaten by heavy seas and groaned and squeaked in every timber, Issy, his eyes wide with fear, would hide in a corner of the sail-room and whisper prayers as he listened intently to the water crashing against the ship's side. He did not go on deck in such weather, having no wish to look at those wild, leaden waves which tossed the old three-decked ship about like a chip of wood and instilled terror in his heart. He preferred to wait out the storm on his own among the sails, coils of rope and lines rather than show himself to people and feel ashamed for trembling and moaning at every violent shudder the ship gave.

But if the whistle blew: 'All hands on deck to take in the fourth reef!', Issy, his heart sinking and cursing his ill-starred fate, would nevertheless rush with the others to the upper deck and haul manfully on the ropes, dashing from place to place and trying not to look at the raging sea. No point in looking at that!

It was at such very rare times that thoughts would come to him of a quiet little corner somewhere on dry land, where he'd be sitting in the warmth on a small stool stitching shoes or boots in the latest style, while his keen, active mind would be full of thoughts about various human and divine matters.

—Better if I'd been put in the army!

Timid himself, he would sometimes look with special respect and a palpitating heart at the topsailmen, who in such stormy weather would run boldly up the rigging, then, like enormous ants, crawl along the yards and, leaning to the white sail, seize its swollen bulk like some invisible force.

—Oof!—he would exclaim, involuntarily expressing both approval and horror lest someone should fall off into the sea or crash down upon the deck, his skull smashed and bloody.

Such accidents happened almost every voyage and always shook him to the core.

And he would hurriedly lower his eyes, look straight down again, and couldn't help saying to the man next to him, as if wishing to pour out his admiration and astonishment:

—Oh, what brave lads! Not afraid of anything!

—Who d'you mean, Issy?

—Them, our sailors!—he would whisper with a feeling of pride for men who were so unlike himself.

IV

But swaying yard-arms and storms frightened Issy far less than floggings and fist-law. Corporal punishments instilled in him not only a panic terror of physical suffering, but an instinctive horror of the shame of violated human dignity. This feeling was highly developed in Issy, as in many Jews, in whose customs there is no habitual recourse to the humiliating punishments which the Russian peasantry of the time had known since childhood.

This dread, which was almost morbidly developed in Issy and made him constantly nervous and tense lest he somehow provoked anger in one of his superiors, had become habitual. Despite 16 years in the navy that had passed safely, he was always on his guard, like a hare which senses the proximity of hounds. After all, in those days when sailors were 'trained' by brutal floggings and when brutality itself was in vogue among sailors, it wasn't hard to come unstuck even with Issy's keen cautiousness!

Issy was unusually sensitive for that age. The sight of a sailor's bared back, the quiet smacking-sound of a flogging administered by angry, sometimes brutalised petty officers or bo'suns, under the keen eye of an officer used to such sights, the body becoming covered with dark-blue stripes with crimson lesions, the man's initially resigned moans which turned into the wild shriek of a defenceless animal and sometimes died away altogether as he lost consciousness—all this filled Issy's heart with indescribable horror and compassion. When he was a witness of such punishments, which in certain instances were carried out in the presence of the whole crew, he could hardly stand on his legs. His puny body would be trembling and he would furtively wipe away tears, terrified lest they be noticed.

It goes without saying that he would never have been present voluntarily at such floggings. When the order was given, after drills or emergencies, for a man to be punished and the white-faced sailor made his way to the foredeck either submissively or with a show of bravado, Issy made his way below to the sail-room. There, blocking his ears, he would agitatedly whisper prayers, anguish in his large, gentle, frightened eyes.

Issy not only sympathised but couldn't help feeling astonishment at the endurance and courage with which many sailors bore punishments which so alarmed him.

He was particularly impressed by one of his close friends, who formed a strange contrast to him. Ivan Ryaboy was a broad-shouldered, thickset man of about 40, a fearless topsailman who went to the very end of the yards—a very difficult and dangerous job. At the same time he was an inveterate lecher and drunkard, and, when drunk, wild and with an unrestrained tongue. Ryaboy was flogged quite frequently, even to the extent that he would bet a glass of vodka that he wouldn't make a sound before 50 strokes. And he really didn't make a sound, but just gritted his teeth, his pale face distorted with pain and anger, and glistening with great beads of sweat. When he'd won his glass of vodka he began shrieking a bit. According to him it made the breathing easier. After sometimes receiving 100 strokes, he'd put his shirt back on and go off as brisk as a bee to smoke a pipe of makhorka. Then he usually went down to see Issy mending sails in the sail-room and said:

—The swines gave me 100, Issy.

—A hundred? O—o—oh!—Issy exclaimed in alarm, though he didn't quite trust his friend's figures, since his cheerful appearance and tone of voice did not correspond in any way to that number of strokes.

—And they didn't half lay them on, I can tell you, Issy. Specially that swine Chekushkin . . . 'cos I was drunk yesterday. They said I'd shot my mouth off at the officer of the watch . . . But I don't remember a thing, so help me . . . You go and prepare your ointment, lad. I'll get someone to rub it on my back.

Issy could make an ointment which, according to the sailors, soothed the pain in the back after punishment and many of them used it.

—I'll prepare it as soon as the whistle goes. The sick-bay attendant will give me the ingredients—he replied and asked almost fearfully:—Does it hurt a lot?

Issy's face wore such a martyred expressed that an observer might have thought that he had been punished, not Ryaboy. His coarse, bronzed face with small, grey, amiably roguish eyes had a look of reckless bravado; it certainly didn't look martyred.

—A flogging, my friend, is meant to hurt! Did you think it wasn't?—Ryaboy answered with a snigger.—But I'll give that swine Chekushkin a bloody face once we're ashore, don't you worry, petty officer or not. I'll smash his lousy mug right in!—the sailor added unexpectedly, a malicious light appearing in his usually good-natured eyes.

—Oh no, Ivanych! What for?

—So the bloody flayer won't try so hard! You beat a man, if that's your swining job, by the rules—you don't lay into him like a madman!

—It'll be the worse for you, Ivanych. He'll get you back later, if you again . . .

Issy tactfully left off there and added with a sigh:

—It's all because of drink.

—Aye, it's drink, Issy. Now you're a brainy fellow, but you can't understand that a sailor's got to have a binge . . . Without it, my friend, he couldn't stand the life. You bear that in mind, Issy.

You're a desperate fellow, Ivanych . . . You're not afraid of anything . . . 100 strokes? Oh, how can you stand it?

—My hide is well upholstered. I've had more than that in my time!—Ryaboy said boastingly.—I shan't grovel before them, the swine, if they tear the skin off me for what I can't remember. I mean, if I shot my mouth off sober, fair enough, flog me to death, but you can't take it out on a man because he was drunk! Is that decent, I ask you?

—Men have long forgotten decency, Ivanych—Issy answered

thoughtfully.

—That's just it. They've forgotten, and I get blind drunk . . . Go on, flog me, if you like . . . Only do it within reason, don't go mad! I'll take 300 and not lie in the sick-bay!

—Go on now!—Issy whispered, looking at Ryaboy with a sort of respectful surprise.

—I don't reckon you'd be able to take 50, would you, Issy? Even that would put pay to you. You're awful puny, Issy!— Ryaboy laughed, looking at Issy's frail figure with the condescending pity of a strong, healthy man.

At these words Issy screwed up his eyes with fear and said in an unusually serious, agitated voice:

—But the shame! You could die of shame alone!

—What shame?—said the bewildered Ryaboy.—That's just your fear talking, Issy! . . If there's any shame, it goes to the man who has no pity and has you flogged for any little thing . . . It's his shame, not the sailor's. God will forgive the sailor all his sins . . . for what he's endured.

Issy never agreed with Ryaboy on this point; here they totally failed to understand each other.

They had both been in the same company on shore and sailed together in summer on the 84-gun *Hasty*, but their relations had been cold, even hostile. The quiet, peaceable Issy, while full of respect for the reckless daring of the sailor who was considered the best topsailman on board ship, was very much put off Ryaboy by his sordid binges ashore, his not particularly delicate ideas about how to get money for his boozing, and rumours to the effect that on dark autumn nights he would leave the barracks and was not averse to robbing a late-returning officer in some dark alley. Ryaboy, for his part, looked on Issy with a certain contempt as a 'dirty Jew' and a dreadful coward as well. However, he never picked on him, considering it below his dignity.

Late one Sunday night after a day's leave Ryaboy was brought back to the barracks unconscious and half naked. He had drunk his way through his boots and his navy greatcoat. Even he felt scared when he awoke the next morning and learned what had happened. Everyone in the company had immediately got to know that Ryaboy had sold government property for drink, and they all said that he'd get a merciless flogging, that they didn't give less than 500 for a thing like that—the coat was new.

The sergeant-major hit him about the ear a bit, more to maintain his reputation than to knock any sense into him—what, he thought, could you teach a man like that!—and promised to hide it from the company commander till the evening, if Ryaboy could procure the coat.

He couldn't even remember how much he'd left it for in the tavern where he always did his drinking. And how could he get it? How could he get the money?

—Looks like I'll have to pay for the coat with my hide, Avdey Trifonych!—he said in a casual voice, trying to hide his real alarm from the sergeant.

—Don't doubt that, you bloody drunken bastard! You'll get a proper going over. They'll go right through your drumskin hide, don't worry. Then, I expect, you'll get a court-martial and end up in the convict squads. How the company commander will look on it, I just don't know . . . It's not the first time you've swindled the navy.

The old sergeant (he was bo'sun of the first watch on *The Hasty*) spoke severely, dispassionately, cursing without any emotion. However there was a sympathetic light in his eyes. This drunken lecher was a fine and fearless topsailman!

—You try and get out of it somehow, you damned bloody devil, and I won't report it till this evening. That's as far as I can go. You know the navy!—he added as if justifying himself.

—Thanks anyway, Avdey Trifonych, but you might as well put it in with your morning report . . . What's the point of waiting?

—Don't come the big man with me . . . You'll get a hell of a flogging . . . And it could be the end of you . . . Or perhaps you haven't woken up yet, you lousy bastard? You hear? I'll not report it till this evening.

Issy had been sitting in a corner working, and had heard about the calamity threatening Ryaboy. His face reflected sympathy and an inner struggle. He sat like that, furiously working his awl, for five minutes or so; finally, he got up with determination and made his way to the other end of the barracks where Ryaboy was sitting morosely.

—Listen to what I'm going to say, friend—Issy said rather mysteriously in his thin, rather drawling voice.

Ryaboy questioningly raised angry eyes at Issy, then lowered them indifferently.

—Know what I'm going to say? . .

—What are you bothering about: 'going to say', 'going to say'? Say it, for God's sake!

—How much did you get for the coat?

—What's that to you? What are you poking your nose in for?

—Just tell me, I've got an idea!—he went on, giving an encouraging and affectionate wink.

—The devil only knows how much if went for.

—Hm . . . You didn't take the money? You just drank it. Did you drink a lot? Couple of litres?

—Aye, and half a barrel more. I'm not a Jew, you know.

—Half a barrel!—Issy gasped.

—What are you getting at, anyway?—Ryaboy asked less angrily now, looking up at Issy and struck by the sympathetic expression on his face.

—I'd like to get your coat back. Just explain where you left it and I'll fetch it.

—You?—was all that Ryaboy could say at first, so moved was he by this magnanimous proposal.

—I won't forget this, Issy! You've got me out of it!—he finally said in a shaking voice and probably wishing to give full expression to his feelings, added:—You're a Jew, yet such a good man!

Issy smiled ever so slightly at this compliment and began asking where the tavern was. Ryaboy gave detailed directions and added with embarrassment:

—Only I expect the landlord will rip you off five roubles more!

On Issy's face appeared the business-like expression of the true Jew about to make a commercial deal, and he gave another wink, this time a rather cunning one.

—I'll likely do some bargaining, I won't give a kopeck more than I have to.

He immediately got leave from the sergeant and set off to the tavern.

The young rogue of a landlord gave Issy a questioning look. He tactfully explained that he'd come for Ivan Ryaboy's coat.

—Have you brought the money?

—How much?

—Seven roubles.—the landlord said without batting an eyelid.

—Isn't that a bit much?—said Issy, screwing up his eyes.

—If you think it's a bit much, you can go.

—I would go, but I feel sorry for my friend . . . You know yourself that it's government property . . . When the company commander finds out you took a piece of government property, there'll be big trouble . . . very big trouble! The police, the lot. Government property cannot disappear.—And Issy shook his head seriously.—Ryaboy told me to give the one and a half

roubles back and ask for the coat and boots. But it's up to you!—
he added with apparent indifference and made as if to leave.

—Just wait a bit . . .

—Sorry, I've no time . . . I'm a navy employee. The sergeant-
major, Avdey Trifonych, sent me himself—do you know him?
He has a drink here too. 'Go and get the coat, Issy,' he said, 'so
there won't be trouble.'

They started bargaining. Issy pretended to leave several times
in his efforts to protect his precious money. He only had about
20 roubles saved up from the 20-kopeck pieces—sometimes it
wasn't even that much—he was given for his work.

The greatcoat and boots were finally bought back for 2 roubles
20 kopecks. When he'd wrapped them into a bundle he went out
in a cheerful, triumphant frame of mind, paying no attention to
the shouts of 'dirty Jew' from the enraged landlord.

From that day on Ivan Ryaboy and Issy became great friends,
though they didn't quite understand each other.

V

In those cruel days Issy needed a lot of intelligence, caution,
resourcefulness and tact to protect himself from punishments for
16 years. But from his very first days in the navy he was so diligent
and conducted himself so irreproachably that it was quite impossible to find fault with him. Besides, one could not help somehow feeling sorry for that mild, timid, puny man with his large
gentle eyes. When during his first year in the service a certain
petty officer gave him a beating with his fists, Issy had wept so
bitterly the whole night that even the man who'd beaten him felt
something akin to pangs of remorse.

Moreover, his unfitness for combatant duty meant that as a
workman he did not come under the eyes of the commanding
officers. He had only two close superiors: the chief bo'sun and
his mate, whom he knew how to get on with and placate when
necessary. The other officers, especially strict with the sailors,
had nothing to do with him. He had only to stay in the sail-
room, mend sails and go on deck during emergencies.

As well as excelling himself in his work and exemplary conduct,
Issy, as an intelligent and perceptive man, also saw other ways of
winning people over. When ashore he was continually making
boots for his company commanders and the sergeants, clothes

for their wives and children, and in the summer did the same for the chief bo'sun and his mate—all for no charge, of course. So they all treated him affectionately, considering him a real find. He could do just about everything. Once he even made a lovely toy which he presented to the son of his regimental commander, for whose wife naturally he was making shoes.

Every day he thanked God that the navy, which he had so feared to begin with, had not proved to be particularly terrible for him—it was just the sea scared him! He didn't have long to do now though. In 4 years or so he would probably be given indefinite leave, and that would be the end of these continual fears! He'd be a free man!

He sometimes dreamed of living permanently on dry land, of plying his trade in Kronstadt where everyone knew him, and earning his living calmly and quietly, as an honest Jew should.

Only one thing had been bothering him of late. He was not indifferent to a sailor's widow who was known in Kronstadt market, where she sold vegetables in summer and various small articles in winter, by the name of 'ginger Anka'. This ginger Anka was a stout, healthy woman of about 35 with broad hips, a puffy, freckle-covered face, and wily, blue eyes, which she would turn provocatively on Issy. Her lover, a sailor, had gone away for three years around the world and she was free. And Issy was a reliable man who gave her excellent business advice. Without him she had hardly enough money for bread and kvas, but after he'd got to know her, things had been very different. Issy was good at business—so shrewd. And he'd made her lovely shoes and loaned her 10 roubles to buy goods.

So Anka wouldn't have minded hitching up with 'the Yid'— never mind if they laughed in the market. They were already laughing, anyway!

Issy, however, made no definite advances, lacking the courage to confess his feelings to her. Besides, would she be willing to live with a Jew anyway? It goes without saying that he didn't even think about marriage.

In all probability the timid Issy would have remained a secret admirer if, one Sunday morning at the beginning of summer when *The Hasty* was already at anchor in the roads, he had not dropped in to buy some onions from Anka. After he'd asked her about business, he was about to go when Anka looked into his eyes and asked archly:

—Is it only onions you want from me, Issy?

—What else could I ask, Anna Spiridonovna?—he replied meaningfully.

—What else? . . Oh, you're an artful one, Issy!—she laughed, and added tenderly:—No point in going back to the ship; you come and have some tea with me!

From then on Issy started coming ashore more often, and when *The Hasty* put to sea, he began making Anka the most fashionable shoes and wrote her two letters in which he eloquently laid bare his heart, ending with advice about the winter business, which they now ran jointly after the memorable purchase of the onions.

VI

The following summer Issy wanted to go to sea less than ever!

He didn't want to part from ginger Anka, to whom he had become seriously attached, but the main thing was that he was worried by the appointment of a new regimental commander as captain of *The Hasty*. Disturbing rumours were going round about him—that he was a terrible bully who, when he'd been in command of a frigate, had had men flogged without pity, and when he got angry he was like a mad dog . . . That was all the sailors were talking about, and even Ivan Ryaboy told Issy one day that he was going to give up drinking . . .

—They say he's an animal!

Indeed, almost every day that summer Issy would run below, trembling with terror. Hardly a single drill passed without a punishment. Sometimes several men were punished at a time. The captain required the sailors to work 'like devils', and if, for example, the sails were furled not in three minutes but in three and a half, all the sailors responsible for the delay were flogged along with their petty officers. In those days speed in the execution of such tasks was a fashion, and every captain wanted to excel. It was a navy craze.

That whole voyage Issy was in a highly tense state and was especially afraid of emergencies, when he too would have to run up on deck and see that tall, broad-shouldered man with a grim red face standing on the quarter-deck, looking menacingly at the work. The sailors did their very utmost, flying up the shrouds like madmen, running out along the yards as if they were on the ground, and furling the sails with the feverish haste of terror. A kind of trepidation was felt by everyone, not excluding even the bo'suns. The officers too stood by their masts with alarmed concern, their heads raised, and occasionally cursed quietly when they noticed that the work was not proceeding quickly enough somewhere or that a rope had jammed.

And that one man who had made everyone tremble was pleased that in two months he'd 'tightened them up' so much. His face lit up with a satisfied smile when the sails 'burned up' or when at artillery drill the great guns rolled back like toys in the hands of the straining sailors . . .

But it also happened—and not infrequently—that the captain's face turned crimson, his eyes bloodshot, and he would rush down to the foredeck in a frenzy with raised fists and hit the bo'suns and sailors who were at hand, filling the air with his curses.

—I'll flog you!—he screamed, beside himself with fury.

It turned out that there'd been loud talking on the foredeck or that the jib-sails had not been furled fast enough. At such moments Issy would freeze in terror.

The voyage was now coming to an end to the joy of sailors and officers alike. *The Hasty* was coming back under full canvas to Kronstadt with a following wind from the Baltic.

Near Gotland a squall hit them and through the negligence of the watch-officer who had not furled the sails in time the fore-topsail was ripped to shreds.

The captain flew into a rage and went for the officer, threatening to have him court-martialled. The whistle blew to change the fore-topsail. The chief bo'sun's mate rushed into the sail-room and in his haste directed the sailors, who had run in, to the wrong topsail, one that needed mending. Nobody noticed this, not even Issy.

About eight minutes later the torn topsail had been unfastened and the one they'd brought—in the form of a huge, long, narrow bag—had been attached in its place. It was unfurled and—oh God!—several holes were gaping in it.

Issy saw them and turned whiter than his shirt.

The captain was already on the foredeck.

—Get the chief bosun's mate . . . and the sailmaker!

The bo'sun's mate and Issy stood before the captain.

—Are you the sailmaker?—asked the captain, boring his bloodshot eyes into the trembling Issy.

—Yes, sir!—Issy could barely mutter.

—You, you scoundrel? Bo'sun! Take him to be flogged! Straightaway!

Issy began to shake as though in a fever. His pupils dilated. His face was convulsed.

—Sir . . . I'm not . . . not to blame.

—Not to blame! . . Hah-ha! . . Take the skin off his hide! . . He's not to blame!—the captain repeated incoherently.

The petty officers had already run up to seize him, when suddenly he fell at the captain's feet and said, sobbing convulsively:

—I can't . . . sir . . . please, I can't . . .

There was something heart-rending in that despairing cry. The first lieutenant who was standing there turned his face away. The sailors lowered their eyes. There was a hushed silence on the deck.

This plea seemed to infuriate the captain even more. He gave the prostrate Issy a kick of disgust and yelled:

—Take him away . . . Let's see if he can't!

But at that moment Issy jumped to his feet. He was no longer his old, meek self; in his deathly pale face and flashing eyes there was something so terribly calm and resolved that the captain took a step back . . .

—A curse on you, you fiend!

With those words he jumped onto the rigging and with a piteous cry of despair hurled himself into the sea.

The sailors froze in silent horror. The captain was obviously taken aback.

Ivan Ryaboy, a fine swimmer, was overboard in an instant. But there was no sign of Issy on the surface! He had gone straight down like a lead weight.

—Damned Yid!—the captain finally said and gave the order to heave to and lower the boat to save Ryaboy.

The sailors were crossing themselves.

The
Missing Sailor

I

T*he Hawk* had been in Hong Kong more than two days now, resting in the calm of the enclosed roads after a stormy passage from Singapore, during which she had taken a thrashing.

Our clipper was black with a small white stripe and she now had the lustre and immaculate cleanliness of a smart warship. The fine lines of her hull, her well-proportioned masts set slightly back with aligned yards and taut rigging would have given pleasure to the most exacting eyes. Thin smoke curled up from the white funnel. This was the fresh-water machine working.

We had a lot of company. Anchored on the roads were an English squadron, warships of other nations, a dozen or so yachts belonging to Hong Kong sportsmen, merchant sailing ships of all imaginable types under various flags, and large awkward-looking junks with dragon's eyes on their blunt snouts.

It was a scorchingly hot morning without a breath of wind. Not a cloud in the sky. The becalmed bay seemed to be melting under the dazzling rays of the burning sun. Very occasionally a light gust of wind would come from behind the mountains, and the flags and pennants that had been drooping in the baking air would flutter and a ripple run across the mirror-like surface of the water.

Despite the suffocating heat there was movement on the water. Numerous sampans with an awning of matting in the middle would be making their way from the city to the ships and back. These sampans glided quickly over the water, controlled very skilfully by a single rower with a scull from the stern, who didn't seem to be put out by the heat.

The sailors, who had just finished swabbing, looked eagerly from the deck at the big, fine-looking, altogether European city with stately buildings among green groves—a city picturesquely situated in the form of an amphitheatre on the side of a large hill on the bare, rocky island.

This island belongs to the English. What had been as recently as the 'forties a bare, deserted rock near the continental mainland is now Hong Kong, the first port in the China Sea, a flourishing English colony and one of the most beautiful cities of the Far East.

On the foredeck no one yet knew when the crew would be given shore leave. The bo'sun Savelyev preserved a meaningful silence, for he didn't know anything himself as the first lieutenant had not given him any instructions. The officers' orderlies had been asked whether they'd heard anything, but had replied that there had not been any talk about it. Thus the sailors had to languish in expectation of shore leave and admire from a distance a city that seemed to promise a full share of pleasure.

The oarsmen on the whaleboat and cutter, who had taken the captain and officers ashore more than once already and had been by the pier, had been able to impart quite precise information regarding the quality and strength of the gin in the nearby inn. Other information, no less interesting for the sailors, was extremely superficial. Their observations on the 'pigtails' (as the sailors called the Chinese) at the pier and their stories about how, apart from rice, they ate 'unclean food' did not particularly interest their listeners, the more so as they had managed to acquaint themselves with the Chinese the very first day they had anchored in the roads.

Hardly had the anchor and boats been lowered when the clipper was surrounded by sampans large and small, like a gang of pirates. Almost immediately, bowing and curtsying, there appeared on deck suppliers, agents, traders, tailors, laundrymen, fruit-sellers, artists—in a word, Chinamen of all descriptions. It was not permitted to let more than 10 men on board, but the Chinese had somehow contrived to slip past the bo'sun and before long there was a large crowd of them on the deck. They blocked the quarter-deck and made their way below, looking into the cabins. Ingratiatingly thrusting their recommendations into the sailors' hands, the traders undid their baskets and bundles to display boxes, tortoiseshell and ivory carvings, fans and fabrics, while the tailors offered to measure or buy ready-made jackets. One man, smiling mysteriously, was advising the officers in abominable English to visit a tea-house and Chinese theatre. An artist was showing samples of his work and trying to persuade a man to have his portrait painted—only 5 dollars. An old, thin, learned-looking Chinaman with tortoiseshell spectacles opened a small bag containing various little files and gimlets and, bending down, pointed to a lieutenant's foot. What could he mean? From his proferred certificate it turned out he was a corn-cutter who performed his operations without any pain at all.

On the foredeck shirtsellers and two hatters were walking about among the sailors. They had bundles of naval uniform caps and shouted:

—Fulyaski . . . Lussian fulyaski!

—The yellow skins have been learning Russian!—the sailors laughed, taking hold of the Chinese by their pigtails and examining the caps.

—How much are you asking?

—One dollar!—replied the Chinaman, holding up a finger for greater clarity.

—Half a dollar?—retorted the sailor, showing half a finger.

The Chinaman was stubborn to begin with, but soon agreed, and several sailors bought new caps.

Meanwhile the crowd had been getting bigger and bigger. The deck had been transformed into a real bazaar. The Chinese were bustling about and shouting. The confused bo'sun Savelyev didn't know what to do. He would drive one or two away but another would appear in their place, or maybe it was one he'd already driven away—they all looked the same.

In the end the captain ordered the Chinese to be put off the ship, for suspicious boats were now lurking under the clipper's prow and bottles being secretively exhibited. The anchor chain could have served as a very convenient supply route.

When he'd received the watch officer's categorical order 'to clean the deck of Chinese', the bo'sun began, as usual, by heaping upon them the most vile and energetic abuse his inventive mind could think of, and then showed them the way off with an eloquent gesture of his hand and the clarifying words:

—Get going, you yellowskins! March!

Though the 'yellowskins' had not properly appreciated the bo'sun's improvisation, his angry appearance and huge fist made them prepare to leave. However, they got ready so slowly, trying to hide from the eyes of the foreign 'barbarian', that Savelyev took a piece of rope out of his pocket. Only then did the frightened Chinese hurry and the deck was cleared. But the sampans paid no heed to the competitive swearing of two bo'suns and several petty officers and did not leave the ship's side. The order then came to fetch the fire-hose and a jet of water dispersed them. But they only retreated to a respectful distance and then stopped.

Only after an hour's vain waiting to be called back and futile attempts by a few of the more daring to approach the ship again did the flotilla finally put back to the city.

On the clipper there remained only one Chinaman, Atoy. He was a bloated, elderly man with small, roguish eyes, who was unusually sedate and apparently impassive in his dandyish, blue-silk gown and new hat with a little black ball. Atoy was the recommended *comprador*, i.e. supplier of provisions. Despite his grave appearance and self-important manners he gave the impression of being a big swindler. His nose seemed to sense spoils.

II

Eight bells sounded and flags were hoisted on all the warships to mark noon. The sailors had lunch and were getting ready to rest when the bo'sun came from the officer of the watch to the foredeck. Planting his long legs wide apart and putting his whistle to his lips, he made his usual grimace, puffed his cheeks and blew. He then shouted cheerfully in a sonorous voice reminiscent of a trombone:

—First Watch ashore! Look lively!

The sailors roused themselves eagerly.

'At last!'—their suddenly bright faces seemed to be saying.

—When is the Second Watch's turn, Maksim Alekseich?—someone asked.

—Tomorrow!—he replied hurriedly and went down to his cabin to smarten himself up before going ashore.

Savalyev liked to cut a dash and swagger in front of foreigners, especially English sailors whom he disliked for looking down their noses at everyone else.

Anticipating the pleasure of trying the much-praised English gin, topsailman Akim Zhdanov was beaming all over his face and put out his makhorka-filled pipe with his gnarled, tar-coated thumb. Shoving his pipe into his trouser pocket he hurried to the ladder and went down to the orlop deck.

With the same cheerful haste he got his sack out of his trunk, took out a clean shirt and trousers, a new pair of boots which he'd made himself from navy stuff, and a dollar wrapped in a piece of rag. He then gave his hands and face a quick wash and started dressing amid a merry, talkative crowd of sailors who were likewise preparing themselves for shore.

Many sailors, those who liked to cut a dash, put on their own shirts with fronts and collars of fine silk, tied at the neck with a black silk kerchief with a metal ring, and put their own tops on their caps. Some even took check handkerchiefs, really just for show. All these articles had been purchased by thrifty sailors from saved 'desert money'.*

Akim Zhdanov had never had things of his own and, it must be said, he even failed to keep navy issue in proper condition. Yet his clothes, while not distinguished by any particular elegance, somehow sat just right on him.

Akim was a short, strong, lean man over 30 years of age, who had served in the navy for more than 10 years. He had a simple, open, not particularly handsome face with a small, broad nose and thick lips partly covered by a clipped moustache. Coarsened and ruddy from wind and rain, and framed by ginger sideburns, his face struck one above all as good-natured and intelligent. His small grey eyes had the same good-natured look too.

His loose-fitting, white linen shirt with a blue turn-down collar which revealed his sunburned, sinewy neck was tied above his trousers with a thick leather belt, from which hung a thin strap to which was attached a sailor's knife, hidden in his pocket. So dressed and with a cap set on the back of his head Akim Zhdanov had the appearance and gait of a fine, hard-slogging seaman, unafraid of any danger. But there was nothing of that showy bravado which sailors sometimes display, especially young ones. Indeed, on the contrary, everything about his small, well-built figure seemed simple and unassuming.

When he'd completed his toilet, Akim took his only dollar from his pocket and looked thoughtfully at the shining coin lying in the broad calloused palm of his hand. A kind of struggle seemed to be going on within him.

He was well aware of his weakness, for which he'd suffered quite a bit—getting blind drunk when he was ashore when he had the money to do it. That was fair enough—why shouldn't a sailor have a good time? But the trouble was that as soon as Akim, to use a sailors' expression, 'took in the fourth reef', i.e. went over his limit, well . . .

He himself rarely remembered what happened then. When he woke up on the clipper without boots or cap, in a shirt torn to

---

* 'Desert money' was money given to sailors who did not drink the wine ration, and money left over after the purchase of provisions.

ribbons, often with a badly bruised face, and on one occasion even in the sick-bay with a nasty knife-wound in his arm, he would cast his mind in vain over the events of the previous day. He would have to learn from his friends that he'd been brought back from shore bound, that he'd 'completely demolished' an English seaman with whom he'd been fighting, and if 'our lads' hadn't come up in time, he'd have 'done in' the man altogether. Or he was told that he'd punched petty officer Lavrentev for no reason, shot his mouth off to the midshipman, and when he'd been lifted from the sloop to the clipper he had bawled for all neighbouring ships to hear that he'd smash them all in.

The sobered Akim would listen to all this information with horror. 'Could it all really have happened?'

But the stern face of the first lieutenant, when he called Akim to account, bore clear witness that it had all happened. And with lowered eyes and a guilty expression on his face Akim would listen to his admonitions and threats, peppered with abuse. Shifting from foot to foot he would every so often utter in a quiet, depressed voice:

—Sorry, sir!

He sometimes had also to endure cuffs about the ears from the enraged first lieutenant, but he still could not promise that 'it' wouldn't happen again. Akim's conscience did not permit him to lie, and he would go to solitary or to the shrouds with the parting promise of a lashing. However, this promise was not always carried out. Corporal punishment was avoided on the clipper, besides which the first lieutenant and the other officers had a certain weakness for Akim as an excellent sailor and a fine fellow.

Indeed, Akim Zhdanov was not only a conscientious, able and fearless sailor but a great lad too. Modest and kind, seemingly incapable of harming so much as a fly, he deservedly enjoyed everyone's affection. They all liked him for his kind, easy-going temperament and his rare uprightness. Everyone knew that he had a heart of gold.

Yet this same kind man would become totally transformed when the drink was in him. He would become a brazen, cursing bully spoiling for a fight; he was ready for any violence, and the wilder it was, the better he liked it. At such moments he seemed to want to enjoy fully an irrepressible impulse to lawlessness, to give expression to an ego which recognised no obstacles, and to show that he was not afraid of anything.

Akim had paid dearly during his service. He had had merciless lashings on the assumption that that would cure him. But the lashings had not cured him. He had held out for a time, but had eventually gone wild again. On the clipper Akim had never been subjected to corporal punishment and they felt sorry for him. This apparently had more effect on him than any punishments, and he would sometimes return from shore admittedly the worse for drink, but not blind drunk and not so wild as he had been before.

—You ought to give up drink altogether, Akim—the bo'sun Savelyev would say to him.—You can't drink sensibly.

—That's right, Maksim Alekseich, I don't know my limit. But I can't give it up.

—You just try.

—I've tried . . . It's no good.

—You'll come to grief . . .

—I know that myself, Maksim Alekseich . . . Anything could happen.

—Get the doctor to treat you. Maybe you've got an illness.

—I was treated by a doctor in Kronstadt. A well-known man he was, Fyodor Vasilich Artemyev . . . He gave me medicine and all.

—What happened?

—It didn't work . . . Looks like the Lord has sent me this ordeal.

—You'd have been a petty officer a long time ago, Akim, but for that one snag.

—I'm not after that, Maksim Alekseich . . . I don't care about being a petty officer. The main thing is the shame of going wild when I'm drunk.

Some officers had also spoken to Akim on the same subject. He usually remained silent with the guilty expression of a man beyond remedy.

III

Full of good intentions not to take 'the fourth reef' that day, Akim hesitated for a few seconds as to whether to take the whole dollar with him, or to get it changed by one of his comrades, leave half on the clipper and have a drink with the other half.

Good sense suggested that he should do just that. He had already been deprived of shore leave anyway for his disgraceful behaviour at the Cape of Good Hope, so that he had had to stay on the clipper while his mates enjoyed themselves in Singapore. After all, he liked having a look at foreign towns and people, and would always take a stroll through a city before going for a drink.

—But perhaps it wouldn't be enough? They say gin is expensive here—Akim pondered.—They might only give me three tots.

Akim was helped out of his difficulty by Vasily Shvetsov. They were both from the same village in Vologda Province, served together on the fore-top, were good friends and usually went about together on shore. Shvetsov would conscientiously take care of his comrade and try to restrain him when he noticed him getting near his 'limit'.

He was a healthy sailor of middle height, with a powerful chest, a ruddy, handsome face, and strong white teeth sparkling behind his red, half-open lips. He was a merry, glib-tongued lad, who loved to fool about and make the sailors laugh, or sing a song and dance the trepak on the forecastle. He was a good sailor but on the lazy side—he knew how to take it easy. He had another weakness; he was a dreadful liar, though he lied with a certain artistic flair and to no real purpose, for he had no intention of harming anyone with his lies. However much they laughed at him, he couldn't restrain himself and at the first opportunity would tell some preposterous lie. He was not averse to drinking when ashore, but he never got drunk and spent more of his money on buying articles and presents for his fiancée, a Kronstadt chambermaid, to whom he wrote long letters filled with fantastic stories about the gales, storms, cities and people he'd seen. The sensitive girl shed many futile tears reading of the horrors and misfortunes dreamed up by her sailor lad.

Shvetsov appeared before Akim all dressed-up.

—What's this, Akim, looking so miserable and staring at a dollar? Sorry to have to spend it, eh?—he asked cheerfully, showing his white teeth.

—That's just it . . . I shouldn't spend it!—Akim said meaningfully.

—You just give it to me to keep, Akim, so as there won't be any trouble, right? Only one condition: do what your friend tells you—not like last time when you gave me a punch in the face! What a man you are!—Shvetsov laughed.

—I'll do as you say . . . You'll be a kind of nursemaid.

—Fine. You and me, Akim, old mate, will have a proper good time, like lords. First, we'll stroll around the town, have a look at the people and the shops, and when evening comes we can have a little drink, not too much, mind you . . . Alright? That would be just fine.

Akim resolutely handed over his dollar and said quietly:

—Look, Vas, don't give me any leeway, be a friend. At the

slightest thing, tie my hands . . .

—Don't worry, old mate, I'll see you through.

—They say drink's dear here?

—There must be all sorts in Hong Kong . . . To suit every taste.

And after a minute's silence Shvetsov suddenly blinked his eyes and blurted excitedly:

—You know what, Akim?

—What?

—We'll be getting shore leave tomorrow too.

Akim knew perfectly well that his friend was lying and said nothing.

—I'm telling you a fact, I am—Vasily went on excitedly.—Makar, the captain's orderly, was just saying . . . The captain himself gave the order to the first lieutenant that every watch was to get two days in a row ashore. He said it was a reward for the sailors' efforts. Makar wouldn't go talking rubbish now, would he?

—You're a good liar, Vas!—Akim smiled.

—Why should I lie? Tomorrow you'll see for yourself. Lie, I ask you!

The sailors standing nearby burst out laughing.

—Come now, lads, Vaska never lies!—someone remarked.

—So we'll be allowed ashore tomorrow too, then?—came someone's voice from the company.

—Definitely!—Vasily insisted.

—Perhaps they'll give us money too . . . You haven't heard anything about that?

—I've only heard what I've heard.

—Just lie away, Vasily Ivanych . . .

Again there was a burst a laughter.

—On deck, lads!—shouted the bo'sun Savelyev as he came up.

The thin, gangling, awkwardly built, ginger-haired Maksim Alekseich was a positively splendid sight. The hair at his temples was brushed forward, his moustache shaved, his sideburns were in the form of cutlets, and he was wearing a thin shirt, squeaky boots and was carrying a multicoloured kerchief in his large, sinewy hands.

—Look lively . . . no point in dawdling! Form up now!—he shouted cheerfully, putting a move behind the lingerers without recourse to his usual oaths.

Soon all who were going ashore were on top.

The first lieutenant was walking along the deck. When he saw Akim, he called him up and said:

—Now watch, Zhdanov. You remember what I was telling you, lad.

—Yes, sir!

—Take care. If you go wild once more, you'll never see shore again. Understood?

—Understood, sir!

—And why are you taking a knife? Leave it behind.

—Yes, sir!

—Well, carry on . . . Let's hope to heaven you'll hold yourself in check, Zhdanov.

Akim took off his knife, handed it to a sailor who was staying behind, and went off for a smoke.

As he did so, the first lieutenant was saying to the bo'sun:

—Savelyev, see that they look after Zhdanov on shore. He mustn't be left alone.

—Shvetsov is always with him, sir. They're from the same place. He keeps an eye on him.

—That's it. Anyway tell them all to look after him.

—Yes, sir!

A few minutes later the order came to get into the long boat, and the sailors filed cheerfully down the ladder.

I had been designated to go ashore with the sailors and bring them back. I had two petty officers to assist me.

Taking his leave of me, the first lieutenant also asked me to take care of Zhdanov.

—You yourself know what a fine sailor he is!—he added.

The long boat was full of white shirts. I climbed down, took my seat by the rudder, and we put off. The steady, rapid stroke of 24 oars soon carried the boat to the landing stage of that beautiful city.

IV

—Back here by seven o'clock—I reminded them as the boat put in.

—Aye-aye, sir!

—Watch now, lads, don't be late. The boat will put off at 7 sharp!

—We shan't be late, sir!

—Ship oars!

The order was no sooner given than obeyed. The boat glided

quietly up to the landing stage and the sailors began jumping hurriedly onto the long-awaited shore.

On the jetty some sailors from foreign merchantmen and English sailors from a sloop-of-war were loitering about, and small groups of Chinese had gathered to gape at the newly arrived foreign guests.

—Lussian, Lussian!—came from various quarters.

Suspicious looking Chinamen were already offering their services. Nodding their heads mysteriously and lisping, they were calling to our men to go with them, explaining in broken English and through gestures where they could have a good drink and a good time.

—Don't listen to them, lads. Send the devils packing!—advised one of the sailors, who'd been in Hong Kong before.—There are plenty of taverns, or rum bars, as they call them here. We don't need that lot to find them. God knows where the devils would take us. When we were here three years ago, they took one of our lads away and let him go in his birthday suit. He got a hiding on the corvette after. What a people! Get lost, you yellow skins!

The advice of the old, experienced sailor worked. The services of the Chinese were rejected.

Several Chinese women with excessively whitened and painted faces were walking back and fore, taking awkward steps on their small, deformed feet. They had rings and copper bracelets on their hands and wrists, and their hair was greased with something or other. They were looking at the newly arrived 'Lussians' from under their paper parasols and smiling sweetly, their narrow eyes darting glances in our direction.

—These Chinese women are alright!—the sailors laughed, looking at them with a degree of interest.

—The bitches are putting on a show for us . . . parading around!

—Slit-eyes, lads!

—Not as good as our Russian girls.

—No comparison!

—Hands off, hands off, Mademoiselle!—a young sailor said in confusion, stepping quickly back from a Chinese woman who had come up to him.

—Scared, Mikheyev?—the sailors laughed.

—Shameless hussy!

—Put your arm round her neck!

At the same place there were palanquins for hire. Tall, strapping Chinese porters with bare shoulders and chests were dozing by them. They woke up and offered to carry me into the city for a half-shilling.

I declined.

—How about trying a palanquin, Maksim Alekseich?—the smartly dressed clerk Skoblikov said to the bo'sun.

—Leave off, will you!—the bo'sun replied scornfully.—Haven't we got legs?

—Yes, but an awful lot of people don't travel on them, Maksim Alekseich. Let's take a ride?

—Not me! I'll travel under my own power.

Not for nothing did Skoblikov admire good form and consider himself a man who understood 'fine manners'. He didn't want to deprive himself of the pleasure of 'taking a ride like the officers'; he climbed rather grandly into the palanquin and sat down, adopting a casual pose, as if to say, 'you can't impress me'. Two sturdy porters took the ends of the long, flexible bamboo poles in their bare hands and bore the delighted Skoblikov uphill at a brisk pace, uttering low shouts to the rhythm of their movement.

—He thinks a pile of himself!—the bo'sun muttered with displeasure.

The sailors split into groups and dispersed around the taverns. There were quite a few near the landing stage and in the lower part of the city, in which were huddled the unsightly houses of the somewhat dirty Chinese quarter. A minority set off for the city, situated on the side of a rocky mountain, to have a walk and a look at the streets, houses and shops before ending the day with a good drink.

Among these inquisitive individuals were, of course, Akim and his friend Vasily Shvetsov.

Despite the scorching heat—it was about 40 degrees—our sailors strode briskly along up the dusty road, exchanging remarks as they went. The sweat was pouring from their reddened faces. Every so often they were passed by palanquins and by coolies who were uttering low shouts and bearing on their mat-covered backs enormous stone slabs, presumably destined for some building or other. Very occasionally they encountered Englishmen in palanquins or on horseback with Indian helmets on their heads. Clearly, only some urgent business could have driven these masters of the island from their cool, comfortable houses at such a hot time of day.

Akim looked with a particular sympathy at the sweating Chinese transporting stone, and finally said:

—The people have a hard time here too, brother.

—What people?—asked Vasily.

—The Chinese. Carrying stone in a heat like this . . . Look, they're carrying sacks over there!

—The slit-eyes have got used to the heat. Look, they go along with shouts . . .

—They do that to catch their breath, so as it'll be easier to carry the load. That's good sense.

After a short silence Akim observed:

—Got used to the heat? You've got to get used to it if you have to earn money for your food. We sailors haven't got it so hard, yet we curse our fate at times. You say: they've got used to it! You just try carrying it!

—No point in feeling sorry for them: they're infidels!—Vasily said contemptuously.

—You're talking rot, Vasya . . . All men are God's children . . .

—Only Christians!—Vasily insisted.

—All men . . . It's written in the books.

—What are you going on for, Akim? Alright, let's say all men.

—Only, the Lord has obviously ordained for the ordinary folk to work and the rich to live in clover. Christian or not, if a man is of plain peasant stock, he has got to work till he drops . . . That's the way it is!—Akim added in philosophical reflection, as if answering his own thoughts.

—Give me capital and I'll live like a lord—Akim laughed.

—God doesn't give capital to the likes of us . . . He loves us. Because with capital men would be finished, that is, if everyone had it . . . Who would look after the land and the corn?

—It ain't half hot, Akimka!—said Shvetsov, obviously not wanting to keep the conversation going.

—Aye, it's hot alright!

They walked on in silence and when they reached the top of the hill they came out onto a large, wide street lined with thick trees. The tall, elegant buildings of offices, hotels and private dwellings stretched right down the street. In the lower stories were splendid shops. Everything was clean.

—A beautiful city!—they both agreed.

They took a rest in the shade of the boulevard, looking at passers-by of all nationalities, and saw an Englishman give a Chinese, who had not stepped aside in time, a stroke of his switch. They swore at this Englishman—one of those knights of profit who go East with the express purpose of making money no matter what, and by whom, of course, one should not judge a whole nation. They then had a smoke of their pipes and went into the first rum-bar and had a large tankard of beer each. Having quenched their thirst, they strolled arm-in-arm around the streets, stopping at the shop windows to gaze at the articles on show. They also went into Chinese shops and in one of them, after much choosing and haggling, Vasily bought a silk kerchief for his fiancée. After this they found themselves in a field in front of barracks. English soldiers were playing croquet on this field and our friends were struck by their clean appearance. About six o'clock, feeling quite tired, they made their way down into the lower city and entered one of the rum-bars not far from the jetty.

A Chinese waiter came up to them.

—Gin!—ordered Vasily.

They sat down at a separate table, drank a tot each and asked for another round. Akim was licking his lips, praising the gin and becoming more excited.

Not far from them sat a group of English sailors.

V

At first Akim poured forth his impressions of the walk around the city. He praised the cleanliness and order in the streets, the beauty of the buildings, the gleaming shops, and was generally of the opinion that Kronstadt could not stand comparison with Hong Kong.

—Not the same 'style', and the English are cleaner than our people.

—They say the English eat a hell of a lot of meat.

—Take their soldiers. You can tell just by looking at them that they are a well-fed lot.

Akim fell to philosophising once again—this time in more detail—about the burden of the Chinaman, and the burden of the ordinary man all the world over. In so doing he tried to work out for himself why the Lord God had so ordained.

Of course it goes without saying that during the whole course of the conversation Akim was busily sipping gin, relishing it like a real drunkard and getting more and more excited.

He was smoking his pipe and talking non-stop, and when he noticed that his glass was empty he said in a slightly confidential tone:

—Let's knock back one more, Vasya. This gin is real good stuff.

—Isn't that too much, Akimka? We've already downed four.

—Four?!—Akim exclaimed in apparent astonishment.— Well, I never, what a light drink! Let's take a fifth one on board, then ship oars! Not a drop more, so as to get back to the clipper in a decent state. I remember my word, my friend! I remember it well, Vas. Don't you go worrying now!—he added with the winning persuasiveness of a sober, lucidly reasoning man, though in fact he was already getting drunk.

Reassured by such sensible words and not noticing his friend's nervous excitement, which was reflected in his inflamed, restless eyes and the impulsiveness of his words and gestures, Vasily was imprudent enough to agree and, imitating the Englishmen, shouted:

—Boy!

The Chinese waiter came up to them. He easily understood what was required, and returned with two filled glasses.

—Look now, Akim, this is the last one!—Vasily said seriously.

—D'you think I don't understand, Vasya? D'you reckon I'm a sailor with sense or not?

—So long as you're sober, Akimka, you've got a lot of sense.

—Am I drunk, I ask you?! Do I look like a drunk man! I'm just enjoying myself. Are we convicts, eh? that we can't have a bit of a binge ashore? Vasya! My friend! take a sailor's life . . . Would you call it good? Remember when they used to flog you mercilessly? Now, thank God, they don't do that . . . I just feel . . . Right, we'll go back decent!

Akim clinked glasses with his friend, downed his gin in one gulp and fell into thought. That glass was, so to speak, decisive. It went to his head. After that glass Akim became a changed man. On his hitherto amiable face appeared a provocative, insolent, drunken sneer. He had now drawn himself up, his head raised, and was looking at his comrade and the English sailors challengingly.

—What did you think then? That I mustn't enjoy myself!—he suddenly shouted with bitter anger.—By what right is that? Travel around all your life and work, but don't have a drink, is that it? Don't give me that, mate! Why can they do it, but not me? . . What sort of sailor am I, Vasya? Tell me honestly what kind of sailor I am. A good one or not?

—A good one . . .

—That's right. I'm a good one and I live decently, so why does the bo'sun throw his weight about? 'Don't drink, Akimka!' he says. And the first lieutenant: 'Don't you dare, or I'll have you flogged.' And tuts his teeth! Alright, flog me! You're a gentleman, and I'm a sort of slave. Beat me, you tyrant! But I'll have a drink ashore anyway, if I feel like it! Flog me, if you want to, I don't give a damn! I'm not afraid of you bastards. Not any of you! I fear the Lord God alone and I'll answer to Him . . . The Lord'll ask: 'Why do you get drunk, Akimka?' I reckon I know what I'll say.

Akim fell silent, then, looking at the bar with its display of bottles, he suddenly exclaimed, recalling for some reason an episode from his pre-Emancipation youth:

—What did they put me in the navy for, eh? By what right? The master fancied my wife. Isn't that the truth of it?

He banged the table with all his strength and shouted:

—Gin!

The impassive Chinese waiter appeared in answer to the summons.

—Akim . . . Akimka! Don't go wild, remember your word!— Vasily tried to calm him, realising that it would be hard to stop him now that he'd 'taken the reef'.

—My word? I'll show you 'word'! Live in bondage and don't enjoy yourself, is that it? Don't bother me, Shvetsov!—he pushed Vasily away.—I'll smash you to pieces!

Despite Shvestov's protests Akim downed one glass after another. There now awoke within him a violent man, clearly looking for a quarrel but not knowing whom to attack. He sat looking suspiciously around him with bloodshot eyes.

At that moment at the table, where the English sailors from a merchant ship were sitting, someone gave a loud laugh and that was quite enough to release the anger that had taken possession of Akim. Before Vasily had time to realise what was happening, Akim was at the neighbouring table. For some reason he chose the strongest, stockiest Englishman sitting there and gave him such a punch on the head that the sailor fell flat on his back.

For a second or two this unexpected attack threw the Englishmen into confusion, but they then immediately began discussing the Russian's action. They clearly considered it highly incorrect and in their turn were about to throw themselves upon Akim, who was standing facing them expectantly, when the man who'd been hit and who had just picked himself up from the floor, said something to them which made them stop. Then the stocky English sailor, looking at Akim with a certain ironic astonishment, gave a wink, pointed to the street and showed him his fists, with which he made movements in the air, as if to say: 'Care for a proper fight?'

Needless to say, Akim expressed his full agreement in immoderately abusive terms.

After settling up for their drinks, the Englishmen and our two sailors went out onto the sea-front and the fighters, surrounded by a circle which was gradually augmented by curious passersby, went into action. It was a hard fight. The English sailor, obviously well-acquainted with the rules of boxing, delivered fairly skilful blows to Akim's chest and face, repelling the wild and disordered assault of his opponent. Akim had already had two teeth knocked out and blood was flowing copiously from his battered face, but, despite Vasily's attempts to get him to leave, he kept going and managed to fracture the experienced Englishman's nose. We don't know how it all would have ended, because the English sailors suddenly took to their heels at the sight of a policeman. A minute later the policeman, who'd come up to Akim, received a hefty punch in the chest.

The policeman, a strong, healthy sepoy, skilfully caught hold of Akim by the scruff of his neck and marched him off in front.

—What have you done, Akimka? You'll be taken to the police station!—sympathised Vasily, not abandoning his friend in his misfortune.

Akim went on cursing, as only a drunk Russian sailor can curse, but then suddenly went quiet and walked on in silence. Presumably, the thought of the shame of spending the night in an English police station had occurred to him, or maybe he simply didn't like being pushed along by some dark-skinned fellow—anyway, he made a sudden movement, tearing himself from the policeman's grasp, landed him a punch and ran off up a narrow alley. The sepoy rushed after him. Nor did Vasily lag behind. But Akim had perhaps a minute's advantage. He turned into a backstreet and suddenly disappeared from sight. He had darted into a Chinese house, whither he had been hospitably beckoned by a rather suspicious looking Chinaman.

The policeman looked for the fugitive for a few minutes, then, turning to Vasily, began telling him something with obvious seriousness, but Vasily didn't understand anything. He hung about in the street for a while, then followed the policeman back to the sea-front quite convinced that Akim would appear in time for the boat.

But the boat came, and there was no Akim.

Shvetsov then gave me a frank report of the whole business. I turned for advice to the policeman who was standing at the jetty.

—It's a serious matter—he said—they could fill him with drink, strip him naked, hand him over to a merchant ship, and he'd wake up at sea.

I took the crew back to the clipper, reported to the first lieutenant and returned straightaway to shore with a letter from the captain to the Chief of Police. That same night I went round the whole Chinese quarter with two policemen, but nowhere could we find any trace of Akim.

—I expect your sailor is already on some merchant ship at sea!—a police official observed.

A tireless search went on for three whole days. All the merchant ships at anchor in the roads were examined on the order of the English Governor.

The captain and officers felt sorry about the unfortunate Akim, to say nothing of the sailors. Everyone was depressed—so well-liked was Akim. His friend, Vasily Shvetsov, was inconsolable, though this did not stop him telling fantastic lies when recounting the circumstances of Akim's disappearance.

Because of the search for Akim we were anchored in Hong Kong ten days instead of the intended six. Despairing of success, we were getting ready to sail, having entrusted the search for the lost sailor to our Consul, when on the eve of our departure Akim was found quite by chance.

VI

This is how it came about.

On the eve of our departure, between twelve and one in the morning, the cutter was bringing some officers who'd been to the theatre back to the clipper, which the previous morning had moved right to the end of the roads, almost to the exit.

Despite the starry sky it was a dark night. Dark and oppressively hot. There was a dead calm, and there were no refreshing puffs of breeze coming from behind the mountains. A deep, sleepy silence filled the roads. The sea seemed to be dozing, as did the numerous ships, visible as tall fantastic silhouettes with the light of lamps twinkling on masts which disappeared into the darkness. Only occasionally, on the half-hour, was the silence broken by the soft, almost mournful sound of ships' bells. Half past twelve sounded, and the bay once more sank into nocturnal silence, amid which only the soft, monotonous and regular splash of our cutter's oars could be heard.

The officers were casually exchanging opinions about the singers of the travelling opera company, which was now going from Hong Kong to Shanghai. Tired from their long rowing the oarsmen leaned more weakly on their oars, taking deep breaths of the unrefreshing night air. It was still quite a long way to the clipper, and her two lights could not yet be seen. The cutter was passing very close to some merchantman with a broad, high prow, when suddenly the silence of the night was broken by a low, sorrowful voice coming from the vessel above us:

—Brothers, help me!

We all shuddered at this unexpected pleading cry. One of the oarsmen said:

—That's Akimka Zhdanov!

English curses could be heard on the merchantman.

—Brothers, hel . . .

The voice broke off suddenly. There was a sound of bustling, then everything was quiet.

Without waiting for an order, the oarsmen stopped rowing and held their oars above the water. They were all obviously expecting to be told to go alongside the merchantman.

—Zhdanov!—the lieutenant, the senior officer among us, called loudly.

There was no answer.

Then he shouted in English:

—On board the merchantman! Is anyone there?

Nobody answered, as if there was not a living soul on board.

After a brief discussion it was decided to go alongside and board the ship in order to free our sailor.

A few oar-strokes and the cutter was alongside.

—What do you want?—came a rough voice from the deck.

—A Russian sailor from a warship . . .

—There's no Russian sailor here.

—We'll see. Wake the captain!—the lieutenant said sharply, and with those words began climbing the ladder. Behind him came we five officers, and behind us six oarsmen. The remaining six stayed on the cutter.

A human shadow disappeared somewhere, and we were left alone on the deck.

—What if they won't give us Zhdanov back?—someone remarked.

—Nonsense! They'll give him back—said lieutenant Gorsky.—

The rogues wouldn't dare otherwise. Any objections and we'll stay put, and send the cutter back to the clipper to let the captain know.

A minute later a tall, square-built, sleepy-looking man came up onto the deck, holding a lamp. He was in a yellow dressing-gown from each pocket of which a revolver was sticking out. He was a curly, dark-haired man in his early forties with an energetic, stern, swarthy face framed by a long black beard.

—What do you want, sir?—he asked coldly, raising the lamp and giving our group a quick glance in which was reflected a degree of morose surprise.

—You are the captain?

—I reckon so. I am the captain, sir, of the American bark *Encounter*. From the Southern States!—he added arrogantly.

It was during the American Civil War.

—And you?—he ended with a question.

—Russian officers from a navy clipper.

The Southerner shook his head in lieu of a greeting.

—To what do we owe the honour?

Gorsky explained the reason for our appearance at such a late hour.

The captain thought for a moment or two.

—You are mistaken, sir . . . I have no Russian here . . . There's all sorts of scum, but there's no Russian, sir . . . You've taken somebody else for him.

—I'll send to the clipper for the crew and make a report to the police!—said Gorsky.

The captain's eyes flashed. He gave a shrill whistle.

A negro sailor appeared in response. The captain hurled abuse at him, promising to teach him a lesson, at which the negro shuddered, and ordered the 'new man' to be fetched.

—I didn't know who they brought me a week ago. I know I paid 15 dollars for him and he tried to run away. So I had him locked up. His nationality was no concern of mine! Those devils of mine shouldn't have let him out at night. By the evening you wouldn't have found a trace of him!—the captain added mockingly.

—You'd have been at sea?

—At sea, sir . . . But now I've got to find another scoundrel! —You've put me to considerable expense, sir . . . I trust you'll recompense me?

—I'll pay you 15 dollars.

—It's not much, but . . . you can't bargain with navy men . . . All right—he added.

A few minutes later Akim appeared in rags, with lesions and bruises on his face. Pale shadowy figures appeared on the deck. The light of the lamp enabled us to distinguish the black, half-black and white, desperate faces of the sailors of that ship.

Meanwhile Akim had rushed to join his shipmates.

—Hello, Zhdanov!—the officers welcomed him affectionately.

—Good morning, sir!—Akim answered in confusion.—God forgive me . . . I nearly sailed with them, sir. It was all my own fault, all because of the drink.

Akim shook hands with his comrades.

Gorsky gave the captain 15 dollars and we started climbing down the ladder.

—God heard my prayers. I'm with Russians again!—Akim said quietly as he sat at the prow.—What I had to endure at the hands of those swine, lads . . . Their captain is a savage beast of a man . . . And the crew . . . collected from all parts . . . Negroes, Arabs, Indians . . . a real hotchpotch!

VII

We raised anchor around midday. When we got out to sea about two hours later a wind sprang up, we shut off the engines and the order came to hoist the sails.

Akim leapt up the shrouds and worked alongside Vasily on his fore-top spar with a sort of frenzy. And when the work was over, he went to the water barrel of the fo'c'sle to smoke a pipe of makhorka, feeling particularly happy to be among his mates, in a group of smoking sailors. Everything round him seemed specially close and dear to him.

He had thought that he would really catch it and had been expecting a lashing. But, to his surprise, nothing of the sort happened. True, the captain had 'shamed' him, and the first lieutenant, having listened to his epic tale with a stern face, had given him a rare dressing-down and forbidden him to go ashore for three months, but all that was nothing compared with the joy he was feeling. Moreover, he felt that the captain, the first lieutenant, and all the officers and crew were glad he was back and held him in affection. The very lightness of his punishment made a deep impression on him. He promised himself that he would not take a drop to drink again. 'It was nearly all up with me!'—he thought with horror.

—Come on, tell us, Akim, how you nearly sailed away with the Americans—the sailors asked on all sides.

—Lads, God spare any man from . . .

—Where did you disappear to in the street when the policeman was chasing you, Akimka?—Vasily enquired.—We looked and looked . . .

—They searched for you for three whole days. The midshipman and the police hunted everywhere. They informed the consul too . . . It was just like the earth had swallowed you up!—remarked the bo'sun who'd come to join them.

—That's just how it seemed . . . Those rotten Chinese lured me . . .

—How d'you like that!

Akim drew on his pipe and went on:

—When I was running from the policeman, a yellow devil beckoned to me . . . He hid me . . . Then, I remember, he brought me vodka. 'Drink', he says in their lingo and gestured. I drank it, and after that I don't remember . . . I came to towards morning . . . I looked round and saw some faces, and there I was lying in the crew's quarters in my birthday suit . . .

—The Chinese took the lot, eh?

—Must have been them. Who else? It was they'd brought me to the merchantship. Well, I was given some rags to put on and taken up on deck with that rabble of a crew grinning and muttering. Their bo'sun, he was white, so I reckon he was American, took me to the captain and said: 'Sailor'. The captain looked a real devil. He gave me a piercing look and said: 'Russian?' 'Russian,'—I replied, and asked to be put back on the clipper, pointing to where she was anchored. But he asked again: 'Russian?' 'Russian!' Then he got a lash from his pocket and cracked it, as if to say, 'that's what you'll get too.' Then he takes out a revolver, threatens me with it and says something to the bo'sun.

—Do the captains have revolvers?

—That one always had one with him. Any sign of mutiny and he'd give you a bullet, lads . . . That's the way it is with them. And the crew were a right desperate lot, I can tell you. Anyway, I was taken below again and shown a bunk, and they were ordered to keep a watch on me . . . My heart went all cold and I nearly wept. I could see it was all up with me.

—You should have slipped away, Akimka!—one of the listeners remarked.

—That's what I was thinking about. I said to myself, I'll unfasten the boat in the night and get away. Well, the night came and I crept on deck. Thank God, the watch is asleep, I thought. I was climbing overboard when that same negro, the watch, I mean, caught me by the neck and started shouting . . . The captain ran out, and I was beaten half-dead, then they put manacles on me and threw me in the hold . . . There I rotted five days, afraid all the time that we'd put to sea . . . Then last night they let me on deck—thanks to the bo'sun—to get some air . . . I was just sitting thinking dark thoughts when suddenly I hear the sound of oars getting nearer and nearer . . . Then I heard Russian voices, so I shouted. That's it, lads, that's how the Lord delivered me. God bless the captain . . . They tell me you stayed here because of me, lads?

—We were looking for you all the time, Akimka.

—Well, I never! The captain is a fine man . . . He couldn't abandon a Russian sailor just like that . . .

—Akim fell silent, then added:

—I'll never take another drop of booze into my mouth again.

—Oh yeh?—someone exclaimed sceptically.

—I swear it, never again!

Among His Shipmates

Soon after the corvette had started on its voyage round
the world, or, as sailors say, 'on the long one', young Ivan
Artemyev, a robust, red-cheeked, handsome, dark-haired
sailor, an intrepid topman and stroke on the captain's whaleboat, caught a chill in the bad weather of the late autumn and
became seriously ill with pneumonia.

The illness dragged on. The young sailor was obviously getting weaker.

When a month later the corvette put into Brest for a few days,
the ship's doctor, a young man who had graduated from Moscow
University some five years previously, once more carefully
sounded and tapped Artemyev's brown chest, which had but
recently been so powerful, but was now wasted, with sharply
protruding ribs. He then made his way to the captain and
reported that Artemyev ought to be drafted off the corvette and
left in the naval hospital in Brest.

—Is he really that ill, doctor?

—Very ill . . . A form of galloping consumption.

—There's no hope of saving him?

—In my opinion none whatsoever!—he answered, with a hint
of that assertive confidence characteristic of very young doctors,
and assumed an even more serious expression.

—It's a shame to send the poor fellow to foreigners to die . . .
But what else can we do? At least he'll be better off on shore than
in our sick-bay. It's not much of a place to be ill in, is it?

—It's not much good for serious cases. It's a small cabin. Poor
ventilation. No facilities.

—That's right. Have you spoken to Artemyev about it?

—Not yet. I'll tell him today, then tomorrow, if you permit,
I'll take him to the hospital myself and hand him over to the
French doctors.

An hour after this conversation the doctor, somewhat agitated but trying to hide his agitation, entered the sick-bay—a small, sparklingly clean cabin located on the orlop-deck. Despite the ventilation hole set in the door, the air was damp and stale, and there was a strong smell of medicines. In the cabin there were four bunks, two along each bulkhead, one on top of the other. Three were empty, and on the fourth, a lower one, his head towards the ship's side, lay the corvette's sole patient, Leading Seaman Ivan Artemyev.

He was lying with dark, shining, wide-open eyes; they were serious with an expression of concentrated thoughtfulness, such as is frequently encountered in those who are suffering a hopeless and prolonged illness. His pinched brown face with its sharp nose, almost transparent nostrils, elongated chin darkened with unshaven bristle, the characteristic burning spots on the sunken cheeks, protruding cheekbones and dry inflamed lips—was calm, handsome and deathly pale. One immediately felt that death was watching over this so recently strong and healthy body.

At the doctor's unscheduled appearance Artemyev slightly raised his head—the hair round his temples was damp with sweat—lowered it again and, playing with the edge of his white cotton blanket with thin, waxen yellow-nailed fingers gave his visitor a frightened and suspicious look.

—Well, old fellow, still feverish?—said the doctor in an artificially familiar and casual tone, supposing that he would thereby cheer his patient up, yet feeling at the same time rather uncomfortable because of the sailor's frightened expression.

—Yes, still feverish, sir! Otherwise I'm all right. There's nothing hurting inside, sir!—Artemyev replied briskly.

And still looking at the doctor with searching, suspicious eyes, he added hurriedly:

—If only I could get rid of the fever I'd regain my strength, sir . . . It's just the fever . . . won't let me.

His hollow voice rang with hope. He was clearly making every effort to seem cheerful and less weak than he was, as though there lurked within him vague suspicions about the doctor's intentions and the sick man wanted to deceive him.

The doctor, a mild, good-natured Muscovite, was not yet so hardened by his profession to regard human suffering indifferently and lowered his head to hide his discomfiture. For some reason he gave a cough and, avoiding the sick man's keen dark eyes, he said in the same artificially casual tone:

—That's just the point, old fellow. The fever's got to go . . . Of

course you'll get better . . . There's no question about it . . .
No question at all.

He stopped for a moment, raised his head and saw the happy,
confident eyes of his patient.

And, despite the heavy feeling that came over him when he
saw that, he went on even more cheerfully and confidently:

—You'll get well, of course . . . You'll be all right again, only
you'll need to go ashore . . . On the corvette, man, you don't
recover as well . . . Understand?

—What do you mean? Ashore?—Artemyev said in an alarmed,
plaintive whisper.

—Here, in Brest, in the hospital . . . It's a very fine one . . .
You'll recover quickly . . . and when you've recovered, they'll
send you to Kronstadt, and from Kronstadt you'll go to your
village, you'll go home . . . I'll give you a certificate for it.

It all sounded very good. But from the doctor's very first
words there appeared in the eyes and on the face of the sailor an
expression of such terror, despair and anguish that the doctor
finished his speech with nothing like the casual cheerfulness with
which he had begun it.

For a moment the patient fell silent, as if struck dumb.

But then he uttered the despairing plea:

—Sir! Please! Don't send me to Brest. Let me stay aboard. I beg you!

The doctor started to reason with him: on shore he'd get
better quickly, whereas here the illness could drag on.

—Sir! Please! . . . If God wills that I don't recover, at least let
me die among my own people, not in a foreign land!

His agitation made him cough. From his chest came an
ominous dull noise, and something inside him gurgled. His
magnificent large eyes looked at the doctor with such pleading
that the young doctor was clearly wavering.

—But listen, Artemyev . . . You'd be better off there!—he
began once again.

—Better off in a foreign land? But I'll die of loneliness there, sir.
Here I've got my own shipmates. At least they'll feel sorry. There's
someone to talk to . . . but there? . . . Please, sir, don't put pay to
me! Let me stay! . . . I'll soon get better, we'll soon be in warm seas
and I'll be a proper sailor again, sir!—he pleaded, as if apologising
for his illness and for not being able to be a good, proper sailor.

Upset by this despair, the doctor realised the cruelty of his
decision and said gently:

—Now, man, don't get upset . . . If you really don't want to go that much, stay here!

A happy, grateful smile lit up Artemyev's deathly face and he said with some emotion:

—I'll never forget this, sir!

The doctor went back to the captain's cabin. He told him of the young seaman's despair and requested leave to keep him on board.

The captain readily agreed and observed:

—We'll soon be in the tropics now . . . Wonderful air . . . Perhaps Artemyev *will* get better . . . What do you think, doctor?

—Unfortunately nothing can save the poor fellow. His days are numbered!—the young doctor replied with certainty and was even rather put out that the captain did not seem to have total faith in his authority.

—What a fine sailor he was!—the captain said ruefully.

II

When they heard on the forecastle—that sailors' club where all events on board are discussed—that Artemyev was to have been sent to a French hospital and had then been allowed to stay on board, all the sailors were sincerely glad for him.

Comments came from all sides:

—If you've got to die, at least it should be among your own people, not like a dog by a stranger's fence.

—Right enough . . . Best straight into the sea!

—Here you're looked after, anyway, but you'd never understand what *they* were babbling about!

—And no priest, no absolution or anything.

—What on earth was the doctor thinking of! Sending him to the French indeed! And he's a good fellow too!

—Aye, he's nice, but . . .

—He's too young, that's it! He's a doctor, but he doesn't even know that a sailor shouldn't die among foreigners. Maybe gentlemen like him wouldn't mind, but a Russian sailor would never willingly agree to it!—was the authoritative pronouncement of the old petty officer Arkhipov, who was puffing away at his makhorka-filled pipe by the water-tub, around which a group had gathered.

And when he'd got it lit, he added categorically:

—That's what it is. He's clever and educated, but he hasn't got much sense. He'll have to learn some, or he'll keep sending men to the French! Way things are, it looks as if our doctor is a bit of a Frenchman himself.

Everyone was silent for a bit, as if they'd found the explanation for the doctor's behaviour. The verdict of such an authoritative person as Arkhipov, whom the sailors greatly respected for his integrity, was, as it were, a resolving chord.

From that day onwards our good ship's doctor was known to the sailors by the facetious nickname 'the Frenchman'.

—Hey, tell us, Ignat Stepanych, mister fielder, sir! Is Vanka Artemyev really, er . . . really going to die?

These words were addressed to the feldsher, the sick-bay attendant, who had just joined them, by the stocky, dark-haired Ryabkin. No longer young, he had a good-natured face, and his bluish nose testified to his chief failing. He was a well-known joker and story-teller, a reckless topman and an inveterate drunkard, who once ashore would drink his way not only through his money but all his possessions too.

The feldsher was a man of about forty, completely befreckled, pockmarked and ugly, who yet considered himself an irresistible Don Juan with the Kronstadt chambermaids. He now assumed a serious contenance, acquired from doctors, put his thumb in the breast of his frock-coat and replied with some assurance:

—Tuberculosis . . . You can't do anything about that, friend.

—Consumption, you mean?

—Pneumonia is one form, tuberculosis—another. Still, you won't understand such wisdom, it's a closed book to you!—the feldsher continued. He loved to dazzle the sailors with various words of that kind.—I can only tell you that poor Artemyev has not long to live.

—You don't say!—Ryabkin exclaimed in alarm.

—I do say! You don't joke with tuberculosis, my friend. It'll see a horse off, let alone a man.

—It's a terrible shame! Nice lad too!—said Ryabkin, and his usual merry smile had gone from his face.

And all who were there felt terribly sorry for Artemyev.

—You're burying him a bit early, aren't you?—said Arkhipov very pointedly.—Perhaps God won't listen to you and the doctor, and will pull the man through.

—What are you going on at me for? I say, live to your heart's content. It's not me, it's science!

—Sci-ence!—Arkhipov drawled scornfully.—The Lord will turn science upside down too, if such be His will . . .

And Arkhipov put his pipe in his pocket and walked slowly away.

The feldsher simply gave a hopeless shrug, as if to say: 'What's the use talking to you!'

III

Two weeks later the corvette was already sailing in the tropics, head-
ing south. The weather was magnificent. Not a cloud in the sky. The
tropical heat was moderated by the gentle, even trade-wind, always
blowing in the same direction, and by the fresh moisture of the ocean.

The corvette went on sailing under full canvas at seven to eight
knots. Not for nothing do sailors call such sailing in the tropics
'holiday sailing'. It is indeed, a calm, happy time! There's no need
to change the position of the sails. Life for the sailors is never more
peaceful. They stand watch, not individually but by sections, and
the watches are very pleasant. You don't have to expect storms or
bad weather, to reef, now hoist, now furl the sails—in a word,
you don't have to be constantly on the alert. On these watches
there is virtually nothing to do. The sailors while away the time by
talking among themselves, recalling their distant homeland.
They are sometimes entertained by the sight of a whale spouting,
or they admire flying fish sparkling in the sunlight, small petrels
flying far from land, huge snow-white albatrosses or frigate birds
soaring high in the clear air. And during those wonderful tropical
nights with myriads of winking stars—nights when the whole
crew sleeps on deck—the men on watch pass the time in small
groups in even more intimate memories or stories told by one of
the skilled story-tellers for the pleasure of his listeners.

The young watch-officer in a white tropical uniform walks
back and fore on the bridge, looking for lights of passing ships.
He takes a deep breath of the cool night air and lapses into
dreams about the past. When tired from his long walking about,
he leans against the rails and dozes with open eyes, as sailors
can. Again he starts pacing, recalling, perhaps, someone close to
him far, far away, or two sweet eyes that seem even sweeter amid
the ocean, or a small hand with long delicate fingers and little
blue veins visible through the tender whiteness of the skin—a
hand which he had but recently kissed furtively in Kronstadt . . .
On these enchanted nights sailors who have not been on land for
a long time become rather sentimental.

The corvette, pitching gently, moves forward in the darkness of
the night, her breast effortlessly cleaving the ocean with a low
rumbling of water sparkling with spray. Behind her she leaves a
broad diamond ribbon, shining with a phosphorescent light.

Occasionally the silent delight of sailing in the tropics is broken
by onrushing squalls with torrential rain. The watch-officer keeps

a sharp look-out for these squalls. Looking through his glasses, he suddenly notices a small grey spot on the distant horizon which had just been clear. It becomes larger and larger and grows rapidly into a dark storm cloud, joined to the ocean by a slanting grey rain column lit up by the rays of the sun. The cloud and the broad grey column are smoving swiftly towards the corvette. The sun has disappeared. The water has grown black. The air is oppressive. The cloud is getting nearer and nearer ... The corvette is now ready to meet its sudden visitor: the topgallant sails have been furled; the topsails, foresail and mainsail reefed ... The squall arrives, enveloping the boat on all sides in grey gloom; it makes the boat heel, carries it for a minute with terrifying speed, drenches everyone in a torrential tropical downpour, rushes further on—and in a minute or two the cloud and rain column become smaller and smaller, until they are but a tiny grey spot on the opposite horizon.

Once again a high blue sky beams down. The air is full of a marvellous freshness. Once more the corvette has hoisted all her sails, and is borne along by the same even, gentle breeze. The sailors' shirts have already dried, and only in the rigging are drops of water still glistening; once again a raised awning shields the sailors' heads from the blinding rays of the tropical sun.

Artemyev seemed to have become better. The fever plagued him at longer intervals, he felt brighter, ate the food from the wardroom with a good appetite and drank two glasses of madeira a day. On the doctor's instructions he was taken on deck in the morning and would spend whole days there, lying most of the time in a hammock, slung near the gangway—on the middle part of the ship. He would watch the usual morning cleaning, pre-lunch duties and drills, listen to the well-known colourful swearing of the bo'sun and the shouts of the officers, exchange a few words with sailors who came to see him—all this engrossed him, being in his eyes a delightful sort of novelty. At times his large, serious eyes would gaze and gaze at the boundless ocean sparkling in the sun and at the high blue sky; he was lost in thought, as if trying to solve some riddle that had unexpectedly arisen for him after his long contemplation of nature and the new, strange thoughts that had appeared during his long illness.

At times his thoughts wandered among memories of his poor far-off village with its dark cottages, of peasant life, of the dark forest where he had often gone at night with his father to cut down 'God's trees', which for some reason were regarded as belonging to the Government—and a great feeling of sorrow came over him then. He felt sorry for his own folk, he grieved over the hard lot of the peasant; he wondered why God was not merciful to everyone, and again he would fall into reflection, looking at the magnificent sky, as though it could provide an answer. . .

Drowsiness frequently overcame him: he would drop off for short periods and have dreams. In these dreams Artemyev was the former strong, healthy, keen sailor, who would climb in one go to the top, furl the topgallant sail or pull hard on his oar, when the captain was to be taken somewhere in the smart whaleboat . . .

Suddenly waking up, he would be sadly aware of his helplessness and look bitterly at his wasted arms, feel his protruding ribs, blame the doctor because he was not regaining his strength, and every morning he prayed with touching simplicity for recovery.

However, there was no recovery in 'the warm seas' either, and the sick man became more and more impatient and irritable. But he didn't think about death, hoping that the fever would finally 'let go' of him and that he would regain his strength.

He was just surprised by the special attention shown to him. The officers and the captain would come to see him and speak kind words of encouragement. Even the cursing bo'sun, who had occasionally clouted Artemyev on the ear, and frequently sworn at him, would look in every so often. And in his rough, hoarse voice there was a surprising note of gentleness, though the bo'sun knitted his brows almost angrily, looking at Artemyev's emaciated face. He would say a few words, and add as he went out:

—Well, lad, get better soon now. No sense in a sailor lying about for long! God is merciful . . . You'll get well.

Everyone, he felt, somehow treated him in a special way.

'Why?'—he sometimes thought, moved by such unusual attention.

Soon the poor fellow learned 'why', when he overheard a careless conversation between two sailors about how the doctor had said he didn't have much longer to live. 'He'll be lucky if he lasts ten days!'

He froze in horror—then he suddenly felt right through himself that it was the truth and that he was not long for this world.

Burning, anguished tears rolled slowly from his fine eyes.

IV

How hard those endless last nights were in the small stuffy cabin! He had virtually no sleep. He would occasionally doze off, then come to again, and lie motionless, with open eyes, in the half-dark room which was dimly illuminated by a lantern. It was quiet all

all around. There was only the light creaking of the corvette and the gurgling of water at its side.

Anguish, gnawing, hopeless anguish!

But Ryabkin, the debauchee and drunkard did not forget the sick man in his nocturnal solitude. Every night, before going on or coming off watch, Ryabkin, depriving himself of sleep, would go into the sick-bay, sit on the floor by Artemyev's bed, comfort and encourage him, and begin telling his endless stories.

He was a really superb story-teller; he had different versions which he'd made up himself, and would tactfully alter the end of a tale, if it were sad or ended with someone's death.

And the young sailor found some comfort in them and sometimes dozed off, lulled by the quiet, rhythmical cadences of the language.

One night Artemyev unexpectedly interrupted him with the words:

—Listen, Ryabkin, there's something I wanted to ask you . . .

—What, Vanya?

—What do you think it will be like in the next world? Will it be hard or not?

Ryabkin, who had never in his life thought about such tricky matters, pondered for a second, but with his characteristic ingenuity quickly found an answer and said confidently:

—I think we can reckon, my friend, that for the likes of us it'll be alright . . . It'll be worse for the masters . . . that's definite . . . because they've got it very easy in this world . . . So they'll go to hell in droves . . . Be our guests . . . This way, gentlemen, please! . . Still, not all of us, either, will go to heaven . . . For example, there's a spell in hell all ready and waiting for me because of the way I drink. Perhaps they'll make me swallow molton bronze . . . I just haven't got the strength to give up the booze, old friend! . . Well, that's how it'll be in the next world!—Ryabkin concluded, apparently absolutely convinced of the correctness of his sudden suppositions.

There was silence for a few moments.

Then the young sailor said:

—Now and again I also wonder: a man dies, and what's there then?

—Will you drop that silly talk! . . . You and me have still got to live some more in this world yet. Last night the bo'sun gave Vaska Skoblikov a hell of a blow! He was bleeding something awful! Right on the nose!—said Ryabkin, abruptly changing the conversation in an effort to distract his comrade's mind from sad subjects.

But Artemyev said nothing and remained indifferent to this information. All the things that had interested him previously did not seem to occupy him now. They all appeared to him to belong to the remote past.

—On your topgallant sail too . . . Mikhaylov forgot to furl the topgallant sail. The mate didn't half let him have it today! But he only hit him once.

Instead of answering Artemyev suddenly said:

—I don't want to die, my friend, but I've got to. It's obviously God's will for me to be thrown into the ocean!—he added with anguish.

—You're just daft! What are you talking nonsense like that for? Do you think I don't know anything about sailors and their health? I know a lot about it, friend. I've been a sailor these twelve years or more . . . On the *Merlin* we had a young seaman who fell ill like you. He was on his back around a year on that clipper, and then he came as right as rain.

But these words did little to console Artemyev. Ryabkin felt this and began his story again.

—You ought to get some sleep, Ryabkin.

—Sleep? . . I don't feel like sleeping . . . I'll get a good sleep in the morning.

—You're sorry for me . . . Kind-hearted, you are . . . God will forgive you the booze!

V

The corvette was approaching the equator. Artemyev was living out his last days.

Early one morning he asked for Yushkov, the midshipman, to come to see him in the sick-bay. Yushkov had earlier been teaching Artemyev to read and write, had often talked to him, written letters for him to his parents at home, and was very fond of the young sailor.

—Sorry to bother you, sir . . . Do me a last favour—write a letter home . . . And the things I'll be leaving, I'd like them sent home when you get back to Russia.

The midshipman started to reassure him, but the sailor stopped him:

—Don't, sir! I know I'm going to die.

And he handed over two gold coins wrapped in a piece of cloth and, pointing to a cotton kerchief, two shirts, shoes, a knitted scarf and some other articles which had been collected on the table, he asked him to send them all to his father and mother.

—Write and tell them, sir, that I . . . that I died, that I was always very mindful of them and in the other world shall pray for them and all the peasants . . . Give my kindest wishes to my sisters and brothers, and the whole village . . . Will you write, sir?

—I'll write!—the midshipman replied, swallowing his tears.

—And write another letter, sir, to Avdotya Matvevna Nikolayeva in Kronstadt . . . And when you get back—give her those presents.

He indicated with his eyes a red silk handkerchief and a small ring with an imitation stone, which he'd bought in Copenhagen.

-—The address is there on the handkerchief . . . Her mother has a stall in the market . . . Write and tell her that she was wrong not to believe me. She thought I wasn't serious . . . and kept laughing. Tell her, sir, that if I did go around with others, it was only because of my hurt feelings; I only ever loved her. Tell her I send my love, kiss her sweet lips and wish her every happiness. Will you do that, sir?

—I'll do it.

—Thank you for everything, sir. Let's say good-bye.

Holding back his tears, the midshipman kissed the sailor's forehead and rushed out of the sick-bay.

That night the young sailor died.

They dressed his corpse in his full naval uniform and early in the morning carried it up to quarter-deck, where they placed it on a board lying on a trestle. Before dinner the priest celebrated a requiem mass in the presence of the captain, the officers and the whole crew. The service and the sad singing of the fine choir amid the boundless, sparkling ocean, so far, far away from home, made the heart ache almost unbearably.

After the service they all went up to take leave of the deceased. The flag had been at half-mast since early morning as a sign that there was a dead man aboard.

As evening came on, the body was sewn in a canvas bag, which completely enveloped it, and a cannon ball was secured to the feet. After the final hymns and naval honours four sailors carried the dead man on the plank to the ship's side amid profound silence, tilted the plank, and with a light splash the young sailor's body disappeared in the clear blueness of the ocean.

They all dispersed in grim silence. Some had tears in their eyes. Ryabkin was weeping like a child.

To starboard the sun was setting majestically, flooding the distant horizon with crimson brilliance.

A Joke

(A Story from bygone naval days)

I

It happened a long time ago.

One hot September day in 1860 the clipper *Darling*, flying the flotilla commander's flag, was making her way up the Yangtse Kiang river from Shanghai to Changchow.

The heat was scorching and the awning overhead was of little help. The sun was blazing down, and the broad, dull-yellow river with its flat banks seemed to be suffocating too.

Every now and again the stokers would run up on deck to be hosed down from the pump. The sailors resting on deck after dinner felt exhausted; they tried in vain to sleep, cursing China and its heat. The sailors on watch were languishing, hardly knowing what to do with themselves. Even the bo'sun Yegorushkin felt so limp that he was not emitting the usual torrents of foul language from his 'cast-iron throat', as the sailors called it, presumably in honour of his ability to curse and consume on shore vast quantities of various spirits, yet remain on his feet and even in full possession of his faculties.

The watch officer, midshipman Vergezhin, was standing on the bridge and melting in his unbuttoned tussore tunic under the scorching rays of the sun, for no awning was permitted on the bridge. He was gazing lazily at the low river-banks and not thinking of anything at all. He couldn't even lean against the rails because they were burning hot. Everything on board was giving off heat.

The midshipman only came to life a little when junks appeared near the prow and he could order whistles to be sounded or the engines to be stopped.

An elderly Chinese pilot with an impassive yellow face stood motionless by the compass. In his katsaveyka and small black cap decorated with a ball he seemed impervious to the devilish heat.

The Chinese pilot, taken on board at Shanghai, was guiding the clipper up-river and hardly ever left the bridge. His name was Atoy, but the sailors inevitably called him 'Atokya' and couldn't get over the fact that the 'pigtail' refused vodka, ate very little, and only rice at that.

Shortly after noon the clipper was passing Nanking, which made Vergezhin lazily recall his geography and look just as lazily at the enormous city with its multitude of pagodas and famous tower.* He then turned away without feeling the slightest desire to be ashore, as he had not been at all impressed by the Chinese girls he'd seen in Shanghai. Besides, he was still greatly affected by the beauty of Miss Kitty, a circus-rider in Hong Kong, with whom two weeks previously he had spent three 'wonderful' days—so wonderful, in fact, that he had drawn his salary for a month ahead and now wore upon his little finger a ring with a precious stone, though of indeterminate type. This and her photograph had been given him by the black-eyed Miss Kitty, a native of Florida, who had generously spent 28 shillings on it out of the £20 bestowed upon her 'for gloves' by the lavish and infatuated midshipman.

—Atoy! Tell me, are the Chinese girls in Nanking beautiful?— Vergezhin asked the pilot in English.

The Chinaman replied quite indifferently in broken English:

—Beautiful.

—Like in Shanghai?

—In Shanghai beautiful, in Nanking beautiful, everywhere young Chinese girls beautiful . . . Must steer more right. On left shallow.

—Steer to port!—Vergezhin ordered.

The clipper's prow veered to starboard.

—That is good!—said the pilot.

—Hold course! Note the compass!—shouted the midshipman.

—Aye-aye, sir!—came the helmsman's voice from below the bridge where the wheel was located.

Some twenty minutes after the clipper had passed Nanking Vergezhin caught sight of great crowds of men on the right bank. There were two crowds separated by a considerable distance and which seemed moving blotches from afar. Among these crowds were to be seen puffs of smoke, followed by the faint dry crackle of gun-shots.

---

* An unique porcelain tower which was destroyed when Nanking was taken by the Imperial forces in 1864.

—Take the glasses, sir!—said the signaller, handing Vergezhin the large naval binoculars.

The midshipman started looking at the shore and could now see fairly distinctly armed men and several horsemen. A battle was obviously going on between those disordered crowds of Chinese.

—Atoy! What's the meaning of that?—he asked.

The Chinaman put his small bony hand with huge, dirty-yellow nails to his eye and looked with apparent impassivity at what he had seen before anyone.

—The Taipings are fighting the Manchus*—he finally said.

Though Vergezhin was little acquainted with Chinese affairs, he had heard and read that for some years now a struggle had been going on in China between the Taipings—as the rebelling Chinese were called—and the government. He knew that the war was being waged with alternating success, that several Southern Chinese cities were under the control of the rebels and that there were many Europeans among their commanding officers.

And Vergezhin recalled the story he'd been told recently by a midshipman from the corvette *Gerfalcon*, which had been in the Shanghai roads at the same time as *Darling*. When the young officer had been in a Ship Chandler's the owner, an old Jew who had emigrated from South Russia a long time ago, secretly suggested to him that he could enter the service of the Taipings as a major and that when he'd signed the contract he'd receive two thousand dollars plus pay of six thousand dollars a year.

—Which ones are the Taipings? I expect it's those with Europeans on horseback in front?—Vergezhin asked, still looking through the binoculars.

—Yes . . . Nearer to us.

A little later he added:

—They will beat the Manchus.

—You think so?

—Certainly. Taipings have Englishman commander.

—Are there many Taipings in China?

---

* The Taiping Rebellion against the Manchu dynasty (1644–1911) lasted from 1850 until 1864. It was largely a peasant revolt but had, at least initially, a strong mystical, quasi-Christian dimension. Spectacularly successful at first, the rebels were soon able to make Nanking their capital (1853). Had they at that time pressed on to Peking, it is unlikely that they could have been stopped. The rebellion was eventually suppressed as a result of the chonic degeneration of the rebel state and the help given to the Imperial government by foreign officers, including General Gordon. (Translator's note)

—Many. All poor people who know why life is hard are Taipings.
—What do they want?
—Better life. Under mandarins it is not possible.
Vergezhin stopped looking at the bank and asked the Chinaman:
—I expect you are a Taiping, Atoy?
—Taiping!—the pilot replied, lowering his voice.
—Why are you not there, with them?
—I have different job. Not everyone has to be soldier.
Vergezhin realised he'd not let the captain know what was happening on the bank and ordered the signaller to inform him that a battle was going on.
—Aye-aye, sir!
The sailor started running to the hatch, but returned almost immediately to report:
—He's coming himself, sir!

II

The flotilla commander and the captain on the *Darling*, both in unbuttoned white uniforms, were coming up onto the bridge.

They had just had lunch and, judging by their florid cheerful faces, sparkling eyes and somewhat unsteady gait, they had lunched very well.

—What's all this, then?—the captain asked Vergezhin. He was an imposing, quite handsome, fair-haired man and was pointing with his small, white and delicate hand towards the bank. His tone of voice was authoritative, as usual, but not unpleasant.

—The pilot says the Taipings are fighting the Manchus.
—Fighting, and you don't let me know.
—I've just sent the signaller.
—It shouldn't have been 'just'—you should have done it when you saw them!—the captain interrupted. He then turned to the flotilla commander with exaggerated politeness, precisely because he didn't give a pin about him, and said:
—A battle, Ivan Ivanych. Those Chinese rogues are fighting among themselves.

The commander of the flotilla, which consisted only of two vessels scheduled to return to Russia, had previously been captain of a corvette; he had then been 'promoted out of the way' by the Admiral commanding the Pacific Squadron. He was a tall flaccid man of about 50 with a large paunch which stuck out

from under his unbuttoned waistcoat and genial face. He gave
a deep, rich laugh, called the Chinese a thing or two, and added:

—I daresay they'll soon run away from each other. Those
scoundrels are cowards!

—Would you care to take a look at them through the binoculars?

The captain handed Ivan Ivanovich the binoculars, and asked
for the telescope.

Ivan Ivanovich planted his legs apart so as to stand more
firmly and, breathing heavily and snuffling through his large
fleshy nose, began looking at the bank.

—They're exchanging fire . . . Frightening each other, but not
coming together. What dolts!—he said and broke into laugher
once more.

It was hard to understand why he was laughing. Was it because
the 'dolts' were exchanging fire, or because at lunch he had not
only consumed three glasses of gin, but had also tried sherry,
lafitte and liqueurs?

The captain too was observing the bank through the telescope.
Suddenly, as if a wonderful idea had occurred to him, he
turned to Ivan Ivanovich and said:

—Will you not permit us to try out our gun, Ivan Ivanovich?

Ivan Ivanovich did not seem to understand what he was
getting at and his large goggle eyes opened still wider.

—How exactly do you mean?

—By sending a shell to the rascals! It would be a fine surprise
for them!—the captain added with a smile, clearly quite carried
away by the idea.

Ivan Ivanovich understood, and the idea appealed to him too
because he gave a merry laugh and, with the affability of a
commander readily complying with a request, declared:

—Well, why not? Why not indeed! Try we will! Go ahead,
Andrey Nikolayevich! Though, of course, only on the rebels . . .
On those . . . What did you call them?

—Taipings, Ivan Ivanych.

—Right. Blow a kiss to the Taipings . . . Let the rascals learn a
bit about kisses, eh? How do we tell which ones are the rebels? . .
Or . . . shall we just . . . leave it to luck?

—I'll ask this blockhead!—said the captain and turned to the
pilot.

The unsuspecting Chinaman pointed with more than a hint of
pride at the crowd he supported, and said:

—They beat the Manchus a week ago. Made them run. And

they will run today.

—What's that he's saying, Andrey Nikolayevich?

—He's hoping the rebels will beat the government forces, Ivan Ivanych. He's obviously a Taiping himnself.

—We'll scare the daylights out of them! . . Ha-ha-ha! Revolt, indeed! Scoundrels.

III

Vergezhin could not believe his ears. Profoundly agitated and disgusted, he looked now at the captain, now at Ivan Ivanovich.

'Are they drunk, is that it?'—he thought. But no! Ivan Ivanovich was noticeably merry, but the captain was merely a bit excited.

'Lord! What are they going to do?'—the young man wondered.

—Vladimir Sergeich! Slowest speed ahead!—ordered the captain.

Vergezhin turned the handle of the engine telegraph.

The *Darling* slowed down.

—Vladimir Sergeich! Summon the gun-crew to No. 1 gun and send for the gunnery officer . . . Open the ammunition room and load the gun with a big charge and a bomb!—he ordered the watch officer distinctly and deliberately.

Vergezhin did not move from the spot but gave the captain a strange look, in which there was reproach and entreaty.

—You heard the order?—the captain asked haughtily, turning his eyes away.

—I heard, but I do not consider it possible to carry out your order, Andrey Nikolayevich!—Vergezhin replied in a barely audible voice, putting his hand to the peak of his cap.

—What's that?—the captain asked in surprise, apparently not understanding what the midshipman was saying.

—I refuse to carry out such orders. Please enter this in the log together with my protest . . . Firing at men . . .

The captain did not let Vergezhin finish. Screwing up his eyes which had gone green with anger, he gave a contemptuous smile and said:

—I'm not interested in your opinion, Mister Vergezhin. Hand over the watch immediately to the relieving officer.

With those words he turned his back on the midshipman.

Ivan Ivanovich, who was standing there, pretended he hadn't heard anything and only gave Vergezhin a sidelong glance.

—What if we get into real trouble, Andrey Nikolayevich?—

he whispered to the captain.

—What for? We'll be firing at the rebels . . .

—Well, I suppose in that case. As allies of the Emperor? . .

—Exactly . . . It's a good chance for firing practice. Pity to let it go.

—Yes, it would be a pity . . .

And Ivan Ivanovich broke into laughter again.

When the officer of the first watch, lieutenant Kichinsky, came up onto the bridge—he had gingery fair hair and his blue eyes had a rather bemused look—Vergezhin told him that he was handing over the watch on the captain's order. When he'd explained what had precipitated the order, he added quietly:

—You refuse too, Vasily Petrovich. It's a disgraceful business . . . You understand? Refuse. You could end up court-martialled . . . You really could!—he was deliberately trying to frighten the timid and weak-willed lieutenant.

But lieutenant Kichinsky looked at Vergezhin distractedly and gave no answer.

The captain ordered him to summon the gun-crew and Kichinsky immediately shouted:

—Bo'sun! Gun-crew to No. 1 gun! Load it with a bomb!

—Coward, coward, coward!—Vergezhin muttered as he made his way from the bridge.

He burst into the wardroom, exclaiming:

—Gentlemen! It can't be possible?!

—What are you so worked up about, Volodenka? Why have you come down?—someone asked.

The agitated Vergezhin hurriedly told them about it.

No one made any reply. There was silence; they all suddenly seemed to feel uncomfortable. Only the elderly doctor finally remarked:

—It's mean alright.

—It's worse than that . . . It's a disgrace . . .

—Don't get over-excited, Vladimir Sergeich! It's not your business to judge the captain's orders. He answers for his actions himself!—the stern-looking but very good-hearted first lieutenant observed pointedly.

—But if his actions are crazy?

—I cannot permit such conversations in the wardroom. I am asking you to stop, Vladimir Sergeich!

With these words the first lieutenant rose from the settee and walked out.

The master-gunner also left, summoned by a petty-officer.

The remaining officers followed them up on deck. Only the doctor and Vergezhin remained in the wardroom.

—What do you make of this, doctor?—exclaimed the midshipman, almost in tears.

—Gun-testing . . .

—The amazing thing is—he's an intelligent and decent man, yet . . . It's just incredible . . .

—Perhaps it's the effect of a good lunch . . . That's probably it.

—And nobody says anything!

—As you see.

—Right, when we get back to Russia, I'm going to resign from the service!—Vergezhin declared decisively.

—And so you should—replied the doctor.

IV

When he saw the gun being loaded, an expression of horror appeared in the eyes and on the yellow impassive face of the pilot. However, the Chinaman regained his composure and seemed to be thinking something over.

—You must keep to left bank . . . To starboard!—he suddenly declared, turning to the watch officer.—It is shallow here . . . Can't go!—he explained.

—Steer to starboard!—lieutenant Kichinsky ordered.

—What is that?—shouted the captain.

—The pilot said . . .

—The scoundrel is lying. He's a Taiping and he's trying to fool us. Keep close to the right bank.

—Aye-aye, sir!

And the helmsman once more put the helm over.

Then the pilot went up to the captain and said:

—I made a mistake, captain . . . I am to blame, captain . . .

—What is it?

—Those not Taipings. That's where Taipings are, captain!—he said, pointing with a trembling hand to the Imperial forces.

—You're lying . . .

—No, captain. I could not see clearly then, but now I see well.

The captain gave a mocking smile.

—Captain . . .

—Get away . . .

The pilot moved away and stood stock-still by the compass.

The gun, which stood forward of the bridge by the mainmast, had been loaded; the master gunner came up to the captain and reported:

—All ready, sir! Where do you want us to fire?

Strangely enough, that question clearly put the captain in some difficulty, and it was several minutes before he replied.

If his head had been at all clouded by drink, it certainly cleared at that moment, and he suddenly saw the idea of sending a shot into the Tapings as a piece of senseless cruelty. However, to cancel the command and order the gun to be unloaded seemed incompatible with his prestige as captain.

Almost all the officers and sailors were on deck. Perplexed, silent and, so it seemed, secretly condemning what was about to happen, they were looking now at the bridge where the commanders were standing, now at the bank from where the sound of gunshots could be heard.

The captain, who guarded his dignity jealously, did not want to appear ridiculous before the ship's company by cancelling the order and thereby seeming to show everyone that he had been alarmed by midshipman Vergezhin's protest. Casting a glance at the deck, he noticed that Vergezhin and the doctor were not there. He understood why, he understood their indignation and was himself experiencing at that moment the heavy feeling of a man who'd got into an impossible position.

But nothing, of course, conveyed his inner torment. He appeared to be completely calm and to know what had to be done.

Then, looking at the bank and measuring the distance with his practised 'sea eye', he finally said quietly to the master gunner:

—Sight the gun at maximum range and aim at the space between the two crowds of Chinese: let's see how far the shot will go.

The way out had been found.

The captain's good spirits had returned and he added with a grin:

—The shot should fall far beyond those scoundrels. So mind now: at maximum range!

—Aye-aye, sir!—replied the elderly, surly master gunner, who seemed rather disappointed.

He came down from the bridge and gave the order to the gunner.

A couple of minutes later the gun had been sighted and ranged. The officer checked it several times himself; sweating profusely, red as a lobster and rather enjoying being the object of general attention, he was now looking at the bridge, waiting for the order to fire.

Silence had descended on the deck—that oppressive silence that inevitably occurs at the sight of something incomprehensible, something that shocks the conscience . . . Almost all the sailors' faces were tense and serious. They all seemed to have the same thought, which sought expression in the question they quietly exchanged:

—We're not going to fire at men, are we?

The cheerful faces of the commanders on the bridge provoked censure.

—Look how rigid Atoyka is standing!—remarked one of the sailors.

—What do you expect? They're going to fire at his people. He's upset.

The Chinese pilot was, indeed, standing stock-still. His pale-yellow face with drawn cheeks had gone yellower still and in its stillness, with closed eyes, seemed lifeless. What was the China-man thinking about as he cursed the 'barbarians', who were ready to commit a terrible act for a joke?

He opened his eyes. They flashed with an expression of hatred and contempt.

V

—You may fire!—the captain said to the watch officer and put the telescope to his eye.

—Fire!—came the order of the watch officer.

All glasses and all eyes were directed at the bank. It was not far away, as the clipper had approached it on the captain's order.

—Fire!—commanded the master gunner.

There was a deafening bang followed by the sharp hissing whine of the projected shell. The gun lurched back. A small white cloud of smoke hung motionless above the ship's side before dispersing slowly in the baking air.

The black ball, which had turned into a barely visible spot, described a long arc and quickly disappeared from sight. Shortly afterwards, far, far beyond the battling forces there was a flash of fire followed by the crash of an explosion.

The deathly face of the Chinaman seemed to come to life again, and the tension suddenly vanished from the sailors' faces.

—So it wasn't at men, then!—an ugly, pock-marked little sailor now said in a loud voice, in which there was a sense of involuntary relief, and crossed himself.

— You thought it would be, you blockhead? Would *he* fire at innocent people?! Not likely! He just wanted the gun tested!— replied another sailor who but a minute previously had not doubted that they'd be shooting at the Chinese. As though feeling guilty for such certainty, he was now defending the captain.

The captain ordered the gun to be secured and its crew dismissed; he then went up to Ivan Ivanovich and said quietly:

— I didn't order them to fire at those scoundrels after all. Let them be! No point in bothering them, dammit!

— Oh, I quite agree!—Ivan Ivanovich replied in happy relief.— Who knows, it might have got back to Petersburg that we treated foreign rebels to a shot . . . Those scoundrels aren't worth our getting into trouble with the High Command.

— That's what I thought, Ivan Ivanych.

— You know what, Andrey Nikolaich?

— What are your orders, Ivan Ivanych?

— I'm not ordering you but asking you, Andrey Nikolaich, not to enter anything about the shot in the log.

— I'll order nothing to be said.

— It's better that way, nothing official. Who knows what might come of it? Why were you firing? What did you fire at the Chinese shore for? And it would transpire that it was because we'd had a very good lunch, Andrey Nikolaich, and excellent wine . . .

Ivan Ivanovich broke into a hearty laugh and added:

— A brandy and soda would go down quite well now. What do you think, Andrey Nikolaich?

— Not a bad idea, Ivan Ivanych.

— Well, come down as soon as you can. I don't intend frying here any longer—said Ivan Ivanych and made his way down from the bridge.

The captain ordered full speed ahead and said to lieutenant Kichinsky:

— Hand over the watch to Vladimir Sergeich. He's still some time to go!

Before leaving the bridge, he went up to the pilot, tapped him on the shoulder and said jokingly:

— Well, Atoy, I expect you were scared for your Taipings, eh?

— I was not afraid for them, captain!

— I'll say you weren't afraid! You tried to get us to fire on the Manchus. You invented shallows near the right bank . . . Go on, admit it, you were scared stiff!

—No, captain. I was quite sure that the Russian generous captain would not give order to fire on foreigners who have done nothing to him!—the Chinaman answered with delicate politeness and as a mark of respect assumed a squatting position.

The captain abandoned his jocular questions and, feeling somewhat embarrassed, went hurriedly down to his cabin for a brandy and soda.

The *Darling* once again moved forward at full speed, cleaving the dull-yellow water of the Yangtse Kiang with her sharp prow. On the clipper everyone was once more languishing in the hellish heat, except Atoy who stood motionless by the compass.

From time to time his yellow face turned to look back at the bank. But soon the clipper rounded a bend in the river and the battle could no longer be seen.

—Tell me, Atoy, will the Taipings beat the Manchus?— Vergezhin asked.

—Certainly!—the pilot answered.

And there was a softer light in his narrow dark eyes when he looked at Vergezhin. Clearly the Chinaman had guessed why the young midshipman had been taken off watch and had not been on deck when the gun was fired.